Jackson's hand brushed against Jojo's as she accepted the important-looking pad. Her pulse jolted. "You really want me to help?"

He kept his hand out and tapped her arm. "Of course. This whole thing is your idea."

"Is it?"

"Well, sort of," Jackson said. "Our idea." Still, his hand was out. Now he was reaching for a handshake. "What do you say? Would you like to become my partner on this?"

Jojo stared at his hand. She felt an electrical charge starting to zoom around inside her. Her head was light, and her knees were wobbly. . . .

**Look for this and other books in the
TOTALLY HOT series:**

point

TOTALLY HOT

#4 Making Changes

Linda A. Cooney

SCHOLASTIC INC.
New York Toronto London Auckland Sydney

ISBN 0-590-44563-4

12 11 10 9 8 7 6 5 4 3 2 1   2 3 4 5 6 7/9

Printed in the U.S.A.   01

First Scholastic printing, February 1992

Making Changes

ONE

Something was still missing from Jojo Hernandez's life.

She had a nice family, including two doting parents, two brothers, and a sister who was away at Northern California State University. She lived in a big house — only twelve blocks from the beach — which had a pool, Jacuzzi, and every kitchen appliance known to man. She had tons of friends at Crescent Bay High, including two best friends, Miranda Jamison, the junior class president, and Kat McDonough, the radio personality. She had decent grades and a position on the cheerleading squad. She also had a perfect smile, dark hair that was naturally curly, bright brown eyes, and a very small waist. Still, something was wrong.

Jojo stood at her kitchen counter, making breakfast for her friends Miranda and Kat. "People may have joked about my being an airhead," Jojo sighed. "But lately I feel like an air person." She waved her arm. "Poof. No more Jojo. Oh, well, she never existed anyway."

She gazed out the kitchen window at the ocean fog that still hung over her yard. She'd been thinking about her problem for some time, and she'd gone through all sorts of theories.

Jojo wondered if it was just that she'd never had a boyfriend. Of course, she'd gone on dates. She'd even thought she'd fallen for newcomer Brent Tucker — for about five minutes. But her romance with Brent had been a joke, just as all her dates had been jokes. Unlike Miranda, who was serious, and Kat, who was funny and intense, Jojo had never been wildly in love or really been passionately committed to anything . . . except maybe to being nice.

Actually, I'll be Miss Flake if I don't hurry up, Jojo reminded herself.

It was a school day and perfectionist Miranda would have a fit if they were one second late to first period. Normally Kat wouldn't care, but Kat had to do her radio show with Gabe Sachs that afternoon, so she probably needed to be on time, too.

Jojo set up the blender and began making the

same breakfast the three of them had shared since the mornings after seventh-grade slumber parties — shakes made with ice cream, milk, and raw egg. As Jojo cracked the egg over the blender, she had this bizarre vision of herself growing up to be a fifties housewife like Wilma Flintstone, wearing a cartoon smile, a frilly apron, and a bone in her hair.

"Nuts," Jojo said.

It was a crazy image, but Jojo was glad to have some far-out thoughts in her head for a change. Jojo wasn't sure why so much of her life had been consumed with mainstream popularity. Maybe it was because she had always been so pampered by her parents that she never looked beyond her locker and her closet.

Jojo poured the shakes into tall glasses and put them on a tray. After that, she began walking gingerly back to her sister's room, where Miranda and Kat were waiting for her. But even before she got past the back door, she realized that something was already happening. Something that hurt, hurt enough to make Jojo stop in the hall outside her sister's old room to catch her breath.

"Haven't you talked to Jackson at all?" she overheard Kat ask Miranda in a fierce whisper.

"Not since the talent show," Miranda whispered back. "What about Brent? Is it really over between you two?"

"Absolutely," Kat swore. "No question."

Jojo stared through the crack in the slightly open door. Miranda and Kat were using their let's-talk-while-Jojo's-in-the-other-room voices again. Miranda was kneeling beside the bed, her hair pulled back in a French braid, her unwrinkled blazer over a high-necked blouse and long skirt. Meanwhile Kat was sprawled on the floor, in a jumper that looked like a clown suit, plus a baseball cap and neon tennies. She wore her trademark, makeshift necklace, which held a swimming nose clip and a pin advertising *Totally Hot*, Gabe's and her school radio show.

"I'll have to talk to Jackson some time this week," Miranda confided. "I have to go to the journalism room and give him the junior class activity report for the next issue of the newspaper." She'd opened her things-to-do schedule and was thumbing through it.

"I'll drop the activity report off for you," Kat offered. "Or ask Jojo. She'll do it."

"Maybe I will," Miranda sighed. "Everytime I see Jackson now this thing happens. It's like this force field comes up and neither of us can say a word."

"It's the same thing with me and Brent," Kat said. "When I see him it's like those magnetic experiments you do in science class, where the magnets push each other apart."

Miranda nodded.

"Brent knows he'd better keep his distance from me now. It's me and Gabe, I guess." A stunned look came over Kat's face. "What am I saying?" She kicked her feet, then buried her face in her hands. "I mean, just me and Gabe doing our radio show! Plus swim team, school . . . and life."

"Maybe it's the life part that's so hard," Miranda answered. She smoothed her blazer. "My dad still bugs me about Jackson, even though I'm not even seeing him anymore. What drives me crazy is that Jackson thinks I wimped out on our relationship because I didn't want to stand up to my dad." She tapped her schedule book against her palm. "Maybe he's right."

Jojo continued to eavesdrop, even though she knew it was something the old Jojo would have done. But she also knew that she wasn't just collecting gossip. She would never repeat a word. But Jojo had missed out on so much already. The previous summer, Kat had had a short, heavy romance with an out-of-town boy. Had she ever told Jojo about it? No. Jojo had been left out again, when Kat had a fling with gorgeous Brent Tucker. And now Kat was back to hanging out with Gabe, doing some friend/romance, off-again, on-again thing. But she didn't discuss that with Jojo, either.

For some reason, Miranda's silence hurt Jojo even more than Kat's. Earlier that fall, Miranda had suddenly broken up with Eric Geraci, the football captain her father adored. Miranda had slipped out of a formal dance to run off with Jackson, the offbeat editor of their school newspaper. But Jojo hadn't even found out about it until things were already over between Jackson and Miranda.

Miranda was staring into her schedule book again, sitting so tall she could have been taking a posture exam. "Well, one thing I'm not going to wimp out on is my Friends in Need counseling," she said.

Jojo wondered if she would ever do something as important as Friends in Need, Crescent Bay High's peer counseling program, where certain students — like Miranda and Jackson — had been trained to help other kids with their problems.

"You won't wimp out," Kat assured Miranda.

Miranda shrugged. "You don't know who I have to counsel."

"And I know I can't ask you who it is, either," Kat told Miranda. "I know how Friends in Need is confidential and all that."

Miranda stared straight ahead. "I can handle counseling him. You survived him, so I guess I will, too."

Jojo stared as Kat suddenly grabbed Miranda's wrist. "Wait a minute. Who is it?"

Jojo inched closer.

"Oh, my God," Kat gasped, clapping her hands to her mouth. "It's Brent."

"No!" Miranda cried. "I mean, yes . . . I mean . . . I can't tell you."

Kat gave Miranda a hard stare. "It *is* Brent, isn't it?"

"Don't tell a single soul," Miranda begged. "I'm not supposed to tell anyone."

"You didn't tell me. I figured it out."

"I have to meet him on Friday night at the Tucker Resort. I can't tell you anything else after this, though."

Kat touched Miranda's arm. "Just be careful.

Brent can be pretty overwhelming . . . when he wants to be."

Jojo was starting to feel overwhelmingly left out. She finally banged into the door with her tray, giving Kat and Miranda plenty of time to change the subject before she stumbled in.

"Here's breakfast," Jojo said. "Sorry it took so long."

"That's okay." Kat quickly jumped to her feet. "I finished setting up the shelf of music and comedy tapes I brought over."

Miranda stood up, too, and neatened her skirt. She pointed to the dresser. "And I finished putting away the books and magazines I brought from home."

"Thanks."

Jojo set down the tray, and they all began to drink their shakes. The only reason she wasn't offended at the swift change of subject was that the new topic was the one thing in her life of which she was truly proud. It reflected the first time she had done something that really mattered.

"You should be excited about this, Jojo," Miranda said.

Kat smiled.

"I just hope it works out," Jojo said as she

glanced around what used to be her older sister's bedroom.

The room would soon have a new occupant. Jojo had asked outsider Leanne Heard to move in, since Leanne had lost her job and her ability to pay rent on her room downtown. After having problems with her mother's boyfriend, Leanne didn't want to return home. "I just hope Leanne talks to me. We're not exactly friends," Jojo admitted.

Miranda checked her watch, then finished her shake. "I don't know if Leanne even talks to Chip."

"Leanne and Chip," Kat sighed. "A couple to set the mind boggling." She picked up her book bag, which was decorated with plastic starfish and dinosaurs. Chip Kohler was another essential person in their crowd, since he was best friends with Gabe Sachs, Kat's partner on the KHOT radio station.

"Well, boggle or no boggle," Kat joked, "we'd better get going if we want to make it to school on time."

Miranda checked her watch and gasped.

"Let's go," Jojo agreed. She downed her own shake and took a deep breath.

Miranda and Kat filed ahead of her, but she

hung back to stare at what would become Leanne's bedroom. Jojo wasn't going to stop here, she decided. Leanne was only the beginning. Jojo's life was changing, and she was on the verge of learning something important and new. And she wasn't going to depend on eavesdropping. She was going to experience it for herself.

Where was Leanne?

Before the first-period bell, Chip was waiting in the second-floor hallway outside the Crescent Bay High chemistry lab. In his tie-dyed T-shirt, baggy pants, sandals, and a ponytail held by a recycled rubber band from the morning newspaper, he looked like his usual laid-back, sixties self. But he wasn't the usual Chip inside. Under the natural fibers and the long hair, he was a wreck.

Why?

Leanne was late.

Had she just gotten held up, or had she finally changed her mind and decided to dump him? Had her mother's creepy boyfriend tossed Leanne into a car trunk, or was Chip just so unimportant that she didn't care how long she made him wait?

"Leanne. Come on. Please. School will start soon."

If they were going to have any time together, Leanne had to show up before the morning crowd, because as soon as other people entered the picture, she freaked.

Chip took deep breaths and tried to count to ten, the way he'd always done to make unpleasant feelings go away. That's when he saw the top of Leanne's platinum hair rising step by step up the staircase. Now there was no need for counting. Nothing but a feeling like helium lightness and exploding joy.

Leanne strode more quickly up the last few steps, then came toward him in a silky thrift-store dress, so long it almost made her trip. When she lifted her pale face and painted red mouth, everything else in the hallway disappeared. The worry. The wait. Even the dusty hall smell was appealing, as Leanne dropped her patchwork velvet bag onto the floor and moved those last few steps.

She slipped her soft arms around Chip's waist. She stood on her tiptoes to kiss the hollow of his neck.

Chip lowered his head to rest his cheek next to hers. His wheat-colored hair, longer and darker than her bleached platinum, fell across her forehead. He touched her unbelievably fine, white skin, then kissed her mouth, feeling as if he were about to melt into the floor.

They kissed and kissed until they heard footsteps down at the other end of the hall. Only when they both knew they had to stop did they finally pull back.

"Where were you?" he managed. She touched his face and looked up at him. His heart was skipping beats.

"Nowhere," she answered, her voice as husky as a rock singer's.

"Nowhere? No one can be nowhere."

"My Ferrari broke down on the way to school."

"Leanne."

"Why are you so concerned with when I get to school and where I meet you?" She let her bleached hair fall over her eyes.

Chip felt a little crack in his heart. He'd fallen so deeply for Leanne, and yet he didn't quite know who she was. Their conversations never felt as connected as when they touched. When they held each other, there was never any doubt. Their hands and mouths were direct lines of communication. "I just wanted to tell you something."

"So tell me," Leanne insisted.

"I want to know if you'll sit with us at lunch today."

"No, I don't want to sit with you." She gave him her tough Leanne look, then melted and got up on tiptoe to wipe lipstick from his neck. "I'd sit with you. But I don't want to be at some crowd table."

"The whole crowd won't be there," he explained. "Kat and Gabe are doing their radio show. That's why I thought today would be good."

"So I get to face just president Miranda. And Miss Popularity Jojo. No thanks."

"In a few days you'll be living at Jojo's house," Chip reminded her.

Leanne shook her head. "Goody for me."

"Jojo's not so bad."

"Not as bad as going back home, so my mother's boyfriend can slug me again."

"Leanne."

She rolled her eyes as the bell rang in Chip's ears. He had to go. His first-period class was on the other side of campus, and he was on probation after getting into a fight with Brent Tucker. He started to turn away.

Leanne caught his hand. "Don't push me," she warned. "I'm just fine the way I am. Just because I have to move in with Jojo doesn't mean I want to become some whole new person."

"I know," he said, pulling her close again, even though he should have been on his way. He couldn't help it. When he was touching her, everything felt so right. But as soon as they let go of each other, their entire relationship seemed to fall apart.

TWO

Kat and Gabe sat side by side in the Crescent Bay High radio station. Spread out before them were the microphone, the volume controls and switches, playlists, and the KHOT sound effects box. Over their heads, the big wall clock ticked away.

Kat caught Gabe's eye and grinned. Since the beginning of lunch her makeshift necklace had held his Walkman earphones. He'd borrowed her pen to write funny messages on her hand. She wore his jeans jacket, while his dark curls stuck out from under her purple baseball cap.

"So radio nerds," Kat said into the microphone.

"Yo, Hot Heads," Gabe crooned.

"I'm sorry to say, it's getting close to the end of today's Totally Hot show." Kat made weepy snorts.

Gabe pointed up to the clock, which was surrounded by Post-its and a few darts. He put on the voice of his favorite radio character, the Lounge Lizard. "But don't despair, all you females out there. I'll be back next week."

Kat replied as Patty Prom Queen. "Not if I can help it."

Gabe pressed the toggle switch on the sound effects box, projecting the sound of a lion's roar followed by a puppy's whine. Gabe slid the final announcement sheet in front of Kat. "To end today's show, we have the ever trusty announcements . . . which we'll have to give you at record speed. Ready . . . set . . . announce!"

Kat clutched the edge of the console.

"ThisFridayFriendsinNeedpeercounselorpro gramissponsoringameetinginthegym, there'sa fundraiserfortheforeignlanguageclub,andthere's goingtobeagirls'athleticconferenceatPoway High!!!"

Gabe panted into the mike.

Kat grabbed a furious swig of Gabe's milk. "Anddon'tforgetthefirstswimmeetnextWed nesdayandtheparent/teacheropenhousenext Fridaynight!"

Gabe wiped milk dribble off Kat's chin, then pointed to the clock again. "We wanted to warn you about the parent/teacher open house in plenty of time," he announced, "in case there's something you don't want your parents to know about."

They were both staring at the clock now, counting off the remaining seconds.

Kat nudged Gabe with her knee. "That's it, Gabe."

Six seconds. He tapped her with his toe. "That's all, folks."

She made a face. "Didn't I just say that?"

Four seconds. "Is there an echo in here?"

"Sign off, Gabe."

"Sign off, Kat."

Two seconds. "We're outta here."

One . . . "WE'RE MELTINNNNNGGGGG GGGG."

Gabe fazed out their volume as he brought up the closing theme song — "Happy traaaaails to . . . ." Then he pressed the applause button, and the sound of uproarious enthusiasm followed.

Quiet.

The red ON AIR light switched off. "Happy Trails" faded away. It was just the two of them in the tiny school studio, surrounded by equipment, shelves of compact discs, notes, food wrappers, dust, and white acoustical tile with the occasional pencil sticking out of the holes.

They both leaned back and enjoyed a post-show sigh.

"Genius burger," Gabe finally said, hooking into their old private lingo.

Kat knew it had been a good show, too. She'd been the strong, funny, together Kat. The Kat who had a direct line from her wit to her mouth. No self-conscious, self-judging, self-stopping thoughts that could be so deadly on the radio. Just patter and jokes that had zinged from her to Gabe and out over the airwaves.

Kat took a mock bow in her chair. Gabe applauded, until she grabbed his hand and pretended to bite it, which made him fall back in his chair, flip around, and drape himself across her lap.

"Yo." He grinned up at her.

Kat's ease began to disappear. Those self-conscious thoughts were coming back. Who is . . . ? What exactly. . . ? Do I want. . . ?

"Kat?"

"Hm?"

"What's up, dudette? What are you thinking?"

All Kat knew was that Gabe was lying across her with his dark curls and green eyes, in his tight black T-shirt, white high-tops, and black jeans. The sensation of him strewn across her lap was making it difficult to think. This wasn't supposed to happen! She'd had enough of losing her head when she'd been seeing Brent Tucker. Finally she was through with Brent. Junior year was supposed to be calm again. But she now felt as calm as a jackhammer.

She jumped up, almost dumping Gabe on the floor. She handed him his earphones and his jacket. As he stumbled into his own chair, she took back her pen.

"Good show, gotta run," she said.

"What's your rush?"

"No rush." She kissed his shoulder, then turned away before he could return the gesture.

"So why are you rushing?" Gabe spun and watched her.

"I'm not."

"Says who?"

"Says me." Her rush was to get away *before something happened!* Lately the Kat/Gabe on-air chemistry was getting an A plus. On the air was safe because the whole school was listening, and it was, well . . . a radio show. But this was the real Kat and Gabe, who had been best friends for a long time. They'd had a few big fights and kissed once. That morning, at Jojo's, Kat had figured it out. She didn't really mind flipping back and forth between friends and something else — as long as she didn't have to pick a permanent side.

Kat grabbed her starfish book bag. "I have my first swim meet next week, in case you don't remember."

Gabe leaned back in his chair and nodded. "I noticed the Popeye bulges in your biceps."

"Ha, ha."

"But you're not going to swim workout now," he bantered.

Of course she wasn't. She worked out before and/or after school in the Crescent Bay public pool downtown. "Well, I have to think about my swim workout."

Gabe stroked his chin. "Think about it. Hmm. Winning through mind control." He closed his eyes, then went into the voice of Mitch Make-It-Up, one of his radio characters. "I think, therefore I win."

"I swim, therefore I'm going," she answered.

Kat knew she'd joked herself into a corner, and Gabe was never one to let her take the easy way out. The only thing to do was take her bag and leave.

"You know, I've been thinking about some

things, too," he said in a serious voice.

She stopped in the doorway. "What things?"

He tapped the back of her knee with his high-top. "You/me. Boy/girl. All of the above."

Kat wanted to scream. "I only believe in true or false!"

He took a deep breath. "So, should we go out sometime? True or false."

"What?"

"Go out. As in date."

Kat's heart was racing again. "Gabe, we go out all the time."

"We hang out. We don't *go* out."

She shrugged.

"How about next weekend?"

Kat wanted to leave that answer blank.

Gabe crumpled up a sheet of show notes and tossed it at her. "You're not still saving yourself for Brent Tucker." He looked down. "Are you, Kat?"

Kat tried to laugh. She wasn't saving herself for Brent. Finally, painfully, Brent was out of her system. At least she hoped so. But she was saving herself for something. Maybe she was just saving herself for sanity.

"No. I'm saving myself for my swim meet," she said. "And next weekend I'm saving myself for that parent/teacher open house thing. On the way to school this morning, I promised Miranda I'd do a Totally Hot routine." She turned back to face Gabe. "Oh. Actually, I promised that *we'd* do a Totally Hot routine." She batted the crumpled ball of paper back at him. "Okay?"

"Okay." He swatted another volley. "Thanks for telling me."

She returned it. "Consider yourself told."

He held the paper ball. "So we'll go out after that."

"We will?"

"If you insist."

"Gabe." Hoping that Gabe just meant the same old go-out-with-the-gang-to-the-Wave-Cafe, Kat grabbed the crumpled paper ball and threw it in the trash. A *date* date with Gabe was too much to think about. So she decided to take the easy tack. She would think about it later.

"I don't know yet. I'll let you know," Kat said, getting up and starting to leave.

"Let me know?" Gabe echoed.

Kat plastered on a panicked smile. "It's okay. It's not until next weekend. We'll figure it out another time." She almost ran into the wall, tripped, but managed to keep her balance. "See you. 'Bye." Then she hurried through the audiovisual room and out into the hall.

" 'Bye," Gabe repeated, almost to himself. "Another time. We'll figure this out another time. Ughhhhhhh."

He watched the clock for a full minute before he pressed a toggle switch on the KHOT sound effects box. The splat of an egg breaking filled the tiny studio.

"Yes, yes," Gabe said to himself. "I definitely laid an egg on that one." He flopped over the console and put his head in his hands. "Whoever thought asking one girl out on one simple date would be so impossible?"

Gabe knew that none of this was really simple. And what he was trying to do was probably impossible. Until recently, he'd been the biggest flirt on the planet. He'd separated girls into two categories: girls to flirt with, and girls who were friends. But now that Kat lived in both camps, he wasn't sure how to handle it. How was it possible to be so close to a girl and have *those* feelings, too?

"Like Chip says, just be patient. Trust in the moment. Things take their own time," he mumbled in a sarcastic voice. "Yeah. Right." Chip might be his best friend, but they were as different from one another as Leanne was from Kat.

Maybe Gabe was no longer the flirt supreme, but he was no laid-back sixties sensitive guy, either. He was still the famous radio deejay voice, the collector of the most classic music cuts ever recorded who lived in a trailer park and had a certain macho image to maintain.

Knock tap tap knock . . .

Gabe spun around again, then took a super-casual pose with his feet up and his arms crossed. He smiled, waiting for Kat to pop in again. She was back to say, okay. Enough. I just want to throw myself into your arms and get this thing settled right now. You're on. We're together. I can't live without you. Simple and neat.

"Come in," Gabe called in a smug voice.

"Hello?" a male voice responded.

Gabe sighed in disappointment, then tipped way back in his chair as the door opened. He immediately recognized Simon Wheeldon, a junior who had freckles, red hair, and was wearing a string tie decorated with steer horns and silver tips. Simon was one of those guys who was so weird that he was almost cool.

"Simon."

Simon peered into the studio, then knocked on the wall outside the door. "Can I come in?"

"You're already in, Wheeler Dealer," Gabe said. Most people called Simon "Wheeler Dealer," because he'd made thousands of dollars one summer running a lawn-mowing service. Simon's business skill was impressive, but Gabe hoped he wasn't dropping by to sell something. As usual, Gabe was flat broke.

Gabe took off Kat's baseball cap and ruffled his hair. "How ya doin'? What's up?"

Simon wore very new jeans, saddle shoes, and a warm smile. Leaning down over the console, he waved a CD case. "I thought you might be interested in this."

Gabe almost jumped up to grab it. "Where'd you get it?"

Simon handed the CD to him. It was called *Sessions With the Greats*. "Just found it downtown." Simon grinned. "Is that the one you were talking about on last week's show?"

Gabe was so excited about the CD that it almost took his mind off Kat. It was rereleased cuts of fifties rock greats, and almost impossible to find. Gabe had raved about it over his show. "Can I borrow it to play next week?"

Simon smiled. "You can have it."

"You just want to give this to me?"

"To the station." Simon stuck his hands into his pockets and rocked on his saddle shoes. "It's a gift."

Gabe knew there was no such thing as a "gift" from Simon. Simon wasn't a bad guy. Actually, he was fairly decent and smart. He was just oriented toward trades and deals. "Come on, Simon."

Simon waved his hands. "Honest, I want to help KHOT."

"Really?" Gabe still didn't believe him. Nonetheless, he slipped the CD out of its case and admired it. "Wow. Thanks."

"Sure." Simon waved and started to leave. "The show today was great."

"Thanks once more." Gabe started to put things away. Even though he was itching to play the CD then and there, it was almost time for class. So he moved quickly, neatening up and making sure all the equipment was turned off.

When Gabe was ready to go he noticed that Simon was still lingering in the doorway. "Simon, I know you want something for this CD. I'd pay you, but I don't have any money."

"Nah." Simon waved his hands. "No, no, no."

"You sure?"

Simon nodded.

But just as Gabe was closing the station door, and strolling through the audiovisual room, Simon seemed to remember something. "Come to think of it, Gabe, there is one little, tiny thing you could do for me. If you want to."

Gabe nodded and led Simon out to the hall. "What's that?"

A blush began to creep over Simon's freckled cheeks. "It's no big thing. I just wanted you to give me some information."

"Information?" Gabe asked.

"Nothing secret," Simon assured him. "I just wanted some hints on how to get to know your friend Jojo Hernandez better."

Simon liked Jojo? And he was going to trade a CD for information about her! Even in his most intense flirting days, Gabe had never resorted to methods like that. And as far as he knew, Jojo wasn't even interested in Simon. Simon and Jojo had sold ads together for the talent show program. Jojo hadn't said anything about him, except that he was kind of a nerd.

"Jojo?" Gabe made sure.

Simon was in full blush mode now. Every

square inch of his face was red. "Jojo."

"What do you want to know about Jojo?" Gabe asked.

Simon stuffed his hands into his pockets. "Well, uh, like is she seeing anybody right now?"

Despite Jojo's popularity, guys didn't usually get crushes on her. Of course, asking Leanne to live with her had definitely given Jojo more mystique. But Simon couldn't know that, Gabe remembered. Leanne wanted the whole thing to be kept hush-hush.

"Nope. Nobody," Gabe said. "Is that all you wanted to know?"

Simon was really starting to sweat. "Actually, there is one other thing. I'd like to get to know her. Could you let me know, oh, if there's anything I can do for her? You know," he stammered, "like helping out the cheerleading squad, or carrying something heavy for her." He scratched his head. "Do girls still like having guys carry heavy stuff for them?"

"Don't ask me," Gabe sighed. He slapped Simon's shoulder. "Anyway, I'll let you know if Jojo needs help with anything."

"Thanks." Simon was getting so red, he was practically on fire. "I'm just trying to make something happen," he explained, wiping sweat from his upper lip. "If you don't make things happen, nothing ever does."

"It's okay, man," Gabe sighed. "I understand." He patted Simon's back again until Simon scurried to join the post-lunch-hall traffic jam.

Gabe stood for a moment while the crowd stampeded past. Not long ago he would have thought it pathetic that Simon had to bribe with CDs just to get a girl's attention. But now that he had such strong feelings for Kat, he wasn't so quick to judge. Who knew what lengths he would go to to get Kat's attention?

After all, he was just trying to make something happen, too.

THREE

By midweek, Jojo doubted that anything really was going to happen at all. She was beginning to feel as if she were back to square one.

"Back to square one," she mumbled. "No. Less than square one. Back to zero."

The only new experiences that Jojo had had so far were her English teacher telling her that she understood symbolism, Simon Wheeldon — of all people — telling her she had mysterious eyes (whatever that meant), and Leanne Heard saying nothing to her at all.

So Jojo just stared into her open locker, hoping to find an answer there.

As she stared, Leanne and Chip slowly came up to Leanne's locker, which was right next to Jojo's. Jojo held her breath. Chip only smiled slightly, which surprised Jojo, since they were really close friends. Meanwhile, Leanne spun her combination lock, leaning into one hip as if she were at war with the entire world.

No one said a word.

Pretty soon Leanne was staring into her locker, too. It was still stuffed with shampoo, perfume, and hair color — supplies for when her rooming house ran out of hot water. Chip stared into both their lockers, shifting from sandal to sandal and eating trail mix.

"This is kind of like staring into the refrigerator when you get home from school," Chip finally joked.

Jojo laughed.

Leanne flinched.

That was when Jojo remembered that Leanne probably didn't have a refrigerator in the tiny room she'd been renting. Chip gave Jojo a sheepish look, as if he'd just remembered the same thing.

But they just kept standing there, staring and feeling weird. They made a strange trio. Jojo in her perky cheerleading outfit. Chip with his blond ponytail and Grateful Dead T-shirt. And Leanne in black karate pants and a man's pajama top, acting as if neither one of them were important people in her life.

Chip tossed Jojo a cashew nut. "Is there a game today, Jo?" he asked, referring to her outfit.

Jojo shook her head. She tried to smile at Leanne. "No. We had our picture taken for some last-minute newspaper thing this morning. I guess they didn't have anything else to put on the front page of next week's issue, so they have to settle for us."

Leanne kept sorting through packs of instant soup, a tin of rice face powder, and a moth-eaten fur jacket.

Jojo looked at Chip again. Then she took a deep breath. "Leanne, I guess you can finally empty all that stuff out of your locker. Since you're about to move in with me, I mean."

Leanne ignored her.

"When are you moving in, Leanne?" Jojo ventured. "Your room has been ready all week. Kat and Miranda helped me fix it up on Monday."

Leanne reacted as if she'd rather climb into her locker and live there.

"Not that I'm rushing you or anything," Jojo backtracked. "You can move in whenever you want. My mom just wanted to know."

"I have one more day in my rooming house."

Leanne shifted. "I don't have to be out until Friday."

Jojo tried not to show how hurt she was. The fact that Leanne would spend every last second in a dumpy rented room, rather than rush over to the big, clean Hernandez house — which even had a pool and a Jacuzzi — was pretty telling.

Chip slowly popped raisins into his mouth. "Jo, I told Leanne about Kat's swim meet," he mentioned, looking back at Leanne. "Maybe we can all go together."

"Gee, thanks," Leanne snapped. "I can hardly wait."

Now it was Chip's turn to try not to look hurt.

"It's got to be more fun than hanging out at the old arcade at the beach," Jojo said, trying to help Chip out.

"Says who?" Leanne tossed back.

Jojo knew she'd really put her foot in her mouth. "Not that there's anything wrong with the arcade," she backtracked, even though Leanne's usual hangouts — the beachfront arcade and old amusement park — were called lowlife and sleazy. "I just mean that swim meets are great. Especially when Kat's competing."

"You ought to know," Leanne muttered. "You're the cheerleader." With that, she slammed her locker door and began walking down the hall.

Chip gave Jojo an embarrassed sigh, then began jogging after Leanne. "Wait up, Leanne," he called. "Leanne! Wait for me. I'll drive you home and help you pack your stuff."

Leanne finally slowed down at the end of the corridor. She and Chip both turned toward the empty auditorium and the last thing Jojo saw was Leanne turning back, then throwing her arms around Chip. Chip swooped her up, pressing his mouth against hers as he spun her around, then ducked into the next corridor.

"I guess you two settled your problem," Jojo said, as Chip and Leanne disappeared.

She was still stung by Leanne's dismissal of her as "just a cheerleader." Maybe Jojo's transformation wasn't taking place anywhere but in her own head. Maybe, no matter how hard she was trying, she still had lightweight, smile queen written all over her.

But then maybe Leanne and Chip were just another couple who had something Jojo would never experience or understand.

*   *   *

Brent Tucker understood plenty. He understood what made a high school operate. Recently, his parents had moved him to the small beach town of Crescent Bay. And Brent knew if he was going to make something of his new life, he was going to have to do it in his new school.

And where better to check things out than in the Crescent Bay High cafeteria. Munching on a peach, Brent cruised. The lunchroom was newly remodeled, but the social games going on were as old as life itself. Who sat where? Who said what? Who was banished to eating lunch alone?

"Brent, Brent! Over here! Eat lunch with us!" cried Brandy Kurtz, the frosty-haired head cheerleader. She was practically leaping onto her table to get his attention. Brent registered Brandy's request, but merely cocked a finger at her and cruised past.

"Hey! Brent, man, come sit with us," a senior jock yelled over the clanging of trays and silverware mixed with echoey laughter. "We saved you a place."

"Later, guys," he called to the jocks. Graceful as a quarterback, he avoided freshmen and food spills. He wasn't about to get ketchup on his pleated khakis, polo shirt, or argyle vest. He was

definitely not someone who went around with
gunk in his golden hair.

Finally Brent stopped under the California flag
to get his bearings. At least the KHOT radio
show wasn't blasting over the cafeteria speakers,
as it had been on Monday. Even though Brent
was through with Kat, the sound of her voice
still grated on him. It reminded him that she'd
been the one desirable girl ever to reject him.
Now he was on a mission to drive a stake
through the heart of her entire crowd.

Brent's blood started to pump faster as he realized that he'd found the something he was
looking for. There it was. Next to some posters
advertising the parent/teacher open house.

The crowd's table.

Brent flinched as he watched Gabe and Kat
giggling and stealing each other's food. Palsy,
as usual. But Jojo's serious brown eyes and dark
curls were anything but usual. Her please-like-
me smile was missing. Instead, she looked
preoccupied and didn't even notice the red-
headed guy in the cowboy shirt who was trying
to get her attention. Brent paused for a moment
and took them all in. Chip wasn't there at all
and neither was Leanne Heard — whom Brent
now lumped with that crowd, because even

though Leanne was an outsider, she was hanging out with Chip.

Brent had begun his mission the previous week, when he'd triggered the fire alarm right in the middle of Leanne's song at the talent show. Afterwards he'd picked a fight with Chip and managed to make Chip take all the blame. He still congratulated himself on the way it had all turned out. Other than Chip, no one knew who had set off that fire alarm. And no one was going to know. Brent wasn't worried about being found out, because he had Vice Principal Hud wound around his finger. And pretty soon, Brent was going to have a member of that crowd wound around his finger, too.

Brent zoomed in on Miranda. She was the only girl in that crowd he hadn't toyed with, and now he wanted her so much it made his heart thump. Gorgeous, overachieving Miranda, with that long hair and that uptight, tall body in her blazers, riding boots, and ruffled shirts. Yes. Brent had already begun his plan, and soon he would start putting it into action.

"BRENT! BRENNNNNNT!!!"

Brent cringed at the voice. It was Brandy again, her megawatt voice breaking through the cafeteria noise. Brent took his concentration away from Miranda, Jojo, Kat, and Gabe, and moved toward Brandy's fourth-quarter scream.

"BRENT! OVER HERE!"

"Okay," he sighed, realizing that he needed a detour before approaching Miranda. It was never wise to approach a girl like Miranda in a straight-forward way. No. Miranda needed phone calls, notes . . . planning. Brent wove through the tables and trays until he found Brandy.

The head cheerleader wasn't alone. A girl like Brandy was never alone, but Brent hadn't re-alized that Brandy was sitting with Lisa Avery.

Lisa and Brandy. What a pair. Lisa had hair the color of polished copper and a body like a Barbie doll's. As usual, she was pushing the dress code to the limit in a neon spandex bodysuit. Meanwhile, Brandy's hair was two-tone frosty brown. Her rail thinness was covered up by a high-necked sweater dress. She had a fake-and-bake tan and eyelashes matted with mascara.

"Hello, ladies," Brent said, as he slid into the chair between them. He took a bite of Brandy's candy bar, followed by a sip from Lisa's diet soda.

"Hi."

Brandy offered him the rest of her candy, but Lisa grabbed her soda back. That was another big difference between the two girls. Like most girls at Crescent Bay High, Brandy drooled over Brent. Not Lisa, though; she hated his guts. Or was trying hard to.

Brent nudged Lisa, hoping to win her over. "Aw, come on, Lisa," he wooed. "You're not still mad at me, are you?"

Lisa glared.

Brent couldn't blame her. Not long after he'd transferred to Crescent Bay High, he'd publicly embarrassed Lisa to score points with Miranda and Kat. And since Lisa was already jealous of super successful Miranda, she'd taken it pretty hard. Brandy, however, was a pushover.

"How are you, Brent?" Brandy asked breathlessly.

Lisa continued to frown.

Brent reached over to examine the dozen or so gold chains draped around Brandy's tiny wrist. "I'm okay." Then he sighed and hung his head. "I don't know. I'm not so great." He continued to touch each chain, making sure to stroke the soft inside of her forearm. "I guess I've been having a hard time lately."

"What's the matter?" Lisa barked. "Did someone finally accuse you of being the two-timing snake you really are?"

Brandy flashed her furry eyes at Lisa.

Brent held Brandy's wrist, as if to say, Leave it to me, Bran. "Look, Lisa," he began in his most sincere voice. "I know you think I double-crossed you when I defended Miranda Jamison. Maybe I did. But I thought I was doing the right thing . . . at the time. I was new. When I first got here, I thought Miranda really was a great person. But first impressions can sure be wrong." He waited to see if his technique was working.

Lisa rolled her eyes.

Brent pushed ahead. "Now I realize that I made a mistake." He sighed. "A big mistake."

Lisa's candy-colored mouth relaxed, but she still looked suspicious.

"I know, Miranda's class president," Brent explained in a softer voice. "Sure, she's a straight-A student, a Friends in Need peer counselor and all that. But there's something about her that bothers me. The more I watch her, the more I feel like something is wrong with this picture."

Brandy was nodding, and Lisa finally began to smile.

"Maybe I'm wrong," Brent hinted. "I don't know. What do you think?"

Lisa stared at him for a moment, sizing him up. He could tell that she still hadn't really forgiven him. Nonetheless, she touched the corner of her glossy mouth and leaned forward. "You know, I date Eric Geraci — among other guys," she bragged.

"I know," Brent said. Everyone knew that Eric Geraci was captain of the Crescent Bay High football team, and that Eric and Miranda had been an item until Miranda had walked out on him in the middle of a formal dance.

"Anyway, Eric really knows Miranda, and you should hear what he says about her," Lisa went on.

"Really?" Brent prodded.

Lisa was still glaring at him. "Well, you know how everyone thinks that Miranda is so strong and independent?"

Brent nodded.

"According to Eric, Miranda is just a wimp," Lisa gossiped. "Her father totally runs her life. Her father tells her that she has to be this supersuccess and do all this stuff at school, and that's the only reason she does it. It's not as if she really cares about her class. And the only reason she dumped Eric for Jackson Magruder was to rebel against her father — for the first time in her life.

She didn't have the guts to tell her father to back off, so she broke Eric's heart instead." Lisa threw a crumpled napkin at Brent. "So there. That's the *perfect*, brave person you stood up for. You creep."

Brent tried to look contrite, even though he wanted to leap up in triumph. This was exactly the kind of info he'd been fishing for! It was all part of his plan. First, he'd found out that Miranda was a peer counselor for Friends in Need. So he'd left Miranda a note, asking for a one-on-one, confidential counseling session — to help deal with his painful rejection by Kat. Now he was planning to psych Miranda out with a little insight of his own. He caught Lisa's eye, but she still frowned at him.

"That whole crowd is so phony," Brandy piped up. "Jojo is the one who drives me up the wall. You know, she's on my cheerleading squad, but lately she's been acting about as spirited as a dead jellyfish. A few weeks ago, she even yelled at *me* for putting down that spooky Leanne Heard."

"Talk about pathetic," Lisa commented.

Brent feigned interest. He'd once found Jojo useful and even flirted with her, but now he was on to other things. He tried not to show Lisa that he'd just become bored.

Brandy twisted her cheerleading charm around her finger. "Something is going on with Jojo and Leanne. I just know it is. My only hope is that when everyone at this school finds out about it, they'll all feel exactly like I do."

"I'm sure you're right, Bran." Brent pushed back his chair. He'd gotten what he'd come for, and he wasn't about to sit around while Brandy raved. Besides, he still had to put in an appearance with the jocks. He stood up and smiled at Lisa. He could tell that he still hadn't completely won her over, but at least she wasn't spitting at him across the table. "It's really great talking to you two. You made me feel a whole lot better. I should get going, though. I've got homework to finish for fifth period."

Lisa scoffed.

Brandy gazed up at him with a dewy smile.

"I'll see you around," Brent said as he backed away.

"You, too," Brandy gushed.

Brent tousled Brandy's hair, then pointed a finger at Lisa. Lisa just stared.

When Brent turned away, he chuckled just a

little. He had no illusions. Brandy was putty in his hands, but Lisa would do what was best for Lisa. If it turned out to be good for him, too, then he would luck out. That was okay, he realized as he glanced at the crowd's table again. He'd gotten what he needed for the moment. And come Friday night he would take what he'd learned and put it to use.

FOUR

The newspaper was not right.

Jackson hunched over his computer and worried. The newspaper was going to press at the end of the week. The stories were almost set, the photos picked out. Everything on the surface looked tidy, organized, neat, the way it should look before he put the paper to bed.

But it still didn't feel right.

The combination of stories was wrong. There were too many light ones, not enough heavy. A photo of the cheerleading squad *was* going on the front page. Where was the hard-hitting news? Scoops. Investigative pieces. He'd transformed *Bay News* into a daring, radical newsheet. But now the paper read like a boring throw away again.

Jackson sighed. "What am I going to do?" he said.

He was alone. As usual, he was the last person in the journalism office on Friday afternoon. The last person to put the newspaper to bed. That was okay with him. He liked the quiet after school. He liked the fact that the only people left in the school were the janitors, the coaches, and the people in the main office. It gave Jackson time to really think.

But sometimes it was painful.

Like this afternoon. Jackson could see that the paper was slipping. And he wasn't sure why. That was the hardest part. He built his staff up for Friday afternoon, convincing them all that they would win some kind of journalism prize. But now that he went through the finished stories one by one, they all added up to one word: *disappointing!*

Lately this had been happening a lot. Worse, Jackson often couldn't fix it. The paper had to go to the printer, even though there would still be stuff that bugged him. He wouldn't have time to start over.

But there was something that bugged him even more. *Miranda!* Jackson was convinced that the newspaper had changed when he started to get involved with Miranda. Even Ms. Hildegard, the journalism teacher, had noticed it.

"The paper feels a little different now," she had told him a couple of weeks ago.

Yeah, it had been different — just like Jackson's love life had been different — for a while. He and Miranda had gone up like a Fourth of July firework. Then just as quickly they had fizzled. Now it was painful to see each other in the hallway. Miranda probably couldn't face him.

"DARN!" Jackson said, bringing his fist down on the desk. The Macintosh did a little blip on the screen, then came back into focus. Not Jackson. His mind drifted back to Miranda — the smell of her hair, the touch of her skin, the kisses they had shared, the secrets.

That was the part that had brought it to a crash — the secrets. Miranda had wanted to keep it that way: secret, private, unknown to everyone but them. She didn't see anything wrong with that, but Jackson couldn't understand. After all, he was the editor of the school newspaper. He believed in dealing with facts straight out. He wanted to tell the truth to everyone. But Miranda was scared of what her dad would think. Also, Jackson was never completely convinced that she accepted him. There was always the underlying hint that Jackson was too much of a free thinker. Too wild. Too out-of-control for straight-arrow Miranda.

And now that's what the newspaper was beginning to remind Jackson of — a paper that was too straight-arrow. A calendar of events; a chronicle of games, clubs, and dances for the kids that were in, but not for the kids that were out.

Jackson got up from his desk and walked over to the large, double window that looked out across the school's front lawn. On the shelf below the window were the two journalism room mascots — a pair of goldfish named Woodward and Bernstein. "Hi, guys," Jackson said.

The fish answered silently. Woodward moved his lips.

"You got any ideas for the paper?"

No answer. Jackson sighed. He thought about Miranda. "You can't make a person something she isn't," he admitted to himself, even though it hurt so much he felt as if he might start to scream.

But he didn't scream. Instead, he did the only thing he knew how to do. He sat back down at his keyboard and began to type.

Even before Jojo could see the open journalism room door, she heard the important, busy sounds. A computer keyboard clacked. A printer thunked.

Jojo hesitated at the top of the stairs. She figured at least she could do a favor for Miranda. Actually, she hadn't even waited for Miranda to ask her to deliver the activity report, but had volunteered for the job. Leanne still hadn't moved in. Chip seemed to be in a haze. Kat was preoccupied with her swim meet, and — if you asked Jojo, which no one did — Gabe was preoccupied with Kat. And in the midst of it all, Jojo was the same old Jojo.

At least the same old Jojo could do a favor for one of her best friends. So she'd walked slowly down the hall, then froze in the journalism doorway. From the noise, she'd assumed that a whole crew of people were inside. But there was only one person there. He wailed angrily on a computer keyboard, while a printer hammered out pages and a news report blared over a portable radio. The lone journalist was Jackson Magruder. He was too involved in his work to notice Jojo.

"Lame," he grumbled.

"What?" Jojo whispered.

"This is still so lame," Jackson repeated, talking only to himself. He pounded the desktop. "This isn't any better than the articles about surfing and the parent/teacher open house. Pathetic. And can't I find anything for the front page besides another picture of cheerleaders?"

Jojo touched the little gold megaphone around her neck and considered walking right out again. But then she reminded herself that she was doing a favor for Miranda. She watched Jackson, who wore a leather bomber jacket. He was slender and graceful. A pencil was propped behind his ear, making his dark hair stick out on that side.

Before Jojo could get his attention, Jackson flopped back over his keyboard again. He pounded the keys, then leaned back, thought, spun around to check something on another desk, muttered, pounded again. If Jojo had only skimmed the Crescent Bay High social waters, Jackson was a deep-sea diver. He always seemed to be connected to things that were real and important.

"Hello?" Jojo finally whispered.

No response.

"Um . . . excuse me?" she said in a louder voice.

Jackson's concentration was so complete that Jojo actually had to back up and bang on the door. When he finally did look up, he didn't flinch or stammer. He didn't even frown at the sight of Jojo's cheerleading uniform. He just looked at her. His eyes were very green and a little sad.

Jojo stared back at him and something sped up inside her. For a moment she forgot why she'd come. "Um. Hi."

"Hi."

She took another step in.

"Do you need something?" he asked.

"Me?" She finally held out Miranda's activity report. "I'm Jojo Hernandez."

"I know."

"I'm a good friend of Miranda's."

A flicker of pain ran over Jackson's face. "I know that, too."

"Oh. I guess you do. This is from Miranda."

He slowly stood up, took the report, then looked past her, as if he expected Miranda to walk in, too.

"Miranda's not here," Jojo said. "It's just me."

"I figured." He scanned the report. Without looking up again, he asked, "How is she?"

"Miranda? Fine. I haven't talked to her all that much since Monday," Jojo babbled. "She's busy working on that parent/teacher open house. She's making the welcome speech. But I'm sure I'll talk to her on the phone about five times this weekend."

Jackson nodded, looked at Jojo for a moment, then sat back at his computer. He placed the activity report facedown, as if just looking at Miranda's signature was too much for him. He didn't pound the keys this time, or curse, or even think. He just sat and stared at his hands.

Jojo rocked on her aerobics shoes, feeling the same way she'd felt when Kat or Miranda wanted to discuss anything important.

"You know, you don't have to put our cheerleading picture on the front page if you don't want to," she offered. "We won't care."

Jackson shrugged.

"Well, the other cheerleaders might care," Jojo clarified. "But I won't."

Jackson ran his hand through his hair, making it stick up.

All the girls had noticed him, even had crushes on him, although he didn't seem to flirt or get involved — until Miranda. There was something about him that spelled out *Special Unique*. He was famous for reviving their newspaper and bringing up unusual points of view at assemblies.

Jackson finally stretched up and turned off the radio. The printer came to a halt, and the room became very quiet. He sighed, stuffed his hands into his pockets, and folded down at his desk again.

"Maybe I just need new inspiration. Or something."

"I know what you mean," Jojo ventured. She had to talk to someone about the way she'd been feeling. And since Kat and Miranda had excluded her, she wasn't about to share her deepest, darkest feelings with them. In the past she might have gone to Chip, but he was too preoccupied with Leanne to have time for anyone else. Still, she wasn't sure that Jackson would be interested. "Or something."

Jackson swiveled in his chair. He gazed up at her with brilliant eyes.

"I guess I've been feeling like I need . . . inspiration, too," she said, encouraged by the brightness in his face. She felt a sudden excitement bubble up inside her, and the fizzy feeling went straight to her mouth. "Or something. I guess I just want to, I don't know, discover something new and important," she chattered. "Sometimes I think it's really important to change, or at least try to change. But it isn't easy. Of course, nothing worthwhile is easy. Right?" She heard her voice bounce back off the walls and blushed. "Do you understand what I mean? Am I making sense at all?"

Jackson was still watching her. "Of course you are."

"Really?" Jojo gasped. "I am making sense? You understand?"

He smiled. "Sure. Change is what it's all about. If you don't change, you die."

"Yes!" She impulsively grabbed a chair and pulled it up next to him. "I agree! You know, I thought I was getting somewhere when I asked this girl in our class to move in with my family. She's been having some problems at home and she's been living on her own. I thought I could help. But now I don't know if I'm doing any good at all. Maybe I never should have asked her."

"Don't say that."

Jojo shrugged. "Why? It's probably true. It is true, I'm sure. It probably won't work out at all."

Jackson propped his chin on his fist. "Who is it?"

"You mean the girl moving in?" Leanne didn't want anyone to know about her living situation, but Jackson was probably the least gossipy person in school.

"Um, it's Leanne Heard," Jojo told him. "Do you know her?"

"I know her." Jackson hiked himself up on the corner of his desk. His jeans were ink-stained and torn at the knees. "Was that your idea, to have Leanne move in with you?"

Jojo nodded shyly.

Jackson smiled, a crooked, smart smile. He reached out and gently touched her hand. "That's great."

Jojo stared down as his skin came in contact with hers. Her heart jumped. Suddenly not a word would come out of her.

"I know that Leanne's had a hard time," Jackson continued. "I also know that it wouldn't be the popular thing to reach out to her." He looked down at his tennis shoes, which had cartoons drawn all over them. "That's a lot more important than what I've been doing with this paper the last few weeks. *Bay News* is getting about as daring as a bubble-gum wrapper.''

When Jackson leaned back in his chair again, Jojo was able to catch her breath. That fizzy feeling was back, making her feel as if she could bounce off the walls. "Well, I just wanted to do something that mattered," she said. "If you really think about it, though, Leanne was the one who really did something first. She was the one who had the courage to get up and sing at that talent show. She's the brave one."

"That's right."

"Of course, then Brent Tucker ruined it all by turning on the fire alarm in the middle of her song," Jojo added, her mouth running away with her. "It was so awful. Horrible! And Chip got in trouble for fighting with Brent about it. And now no one will ever know that it was all Brent's fault."

Jackson jumped away from his desk and moved toward Jojo. His face was only inches from hers. "Wait a minute, Jojo. Slow down. Back up." He was the old, quirky, intense Jackson again. "Brent Tucker set off that fire alarm during the talent show?" He grabbed her shoulders.

Again Jojo stared at his hands. First one, then

the other, wound around her slender arms. "Uh-huh," she breathed.

"Are you sure?"

"I'm sure. Chip saw Brent do it."

"He did?"

Jojo felt as if she'd gone into another reality. All the right words were coming out, but everything was framed by the overwhelming feeling of Jackson's hands. "And then Chip got in trouble with Hud, while Brent walked away scot-free."

Jackson let her go, grabbed a pencil from behind his ear, and began scribbling on a pad. "Did anyone else see?"

Jojo almost collapsed, as if he had been holding her up. "I . . . don't . . . know. Why?"

Jackson was scribbling like a maniac now. "I've been wanting to do a real investigative piece for a long time. This is just what the paper needs."

It took Jojo a moment to realize what Jackson was talking about. An investigative piece? "You want to expose Brent Tucker in the paper?"

Jackson lifted his face and grinned.

His smile made Jojo feel like the sun had suddenly come out. "Can you really do it?"

"Only if I have help. We'll need more proof,"
he said. "We'll need another eye witness. People
will think Chip is just defending himself. We
have to find somebody besides Chip who saw
Brent pull that alarm."

Jojo's heart began to pound. "We?"

Jackson kept writing.

"But . . . I mean . . . how will we find another
witness?" she asked.

"We'll look. You know more of those people
who were in the talent show than I do. Talk to
all of them." Jackson quickly handed Jojo a
newspaper pad and pen. Once more, his hand
touched hers. "Find out if anybody else happened to walk by and see Tucker pull that
switch. Use this for notes."

"What?"

"Take notes. Keep track of everyone you talk
to. Be discreet."

Jojo slowly accepted the important-looking
pad, stretching out the moment when their fingers touched. She looked right at him. "You
really want me to help?" she whispered.

He nudged her. "Of course. This whole thing
is your idea."

"It is?"

"Well, sort of," Jackson said. "Our idea."

Jojo realized that he'd moved his hand and was now reaching for a handshake. She stared down at his palm.

"What do you say?" Jackson asked. "Would you like to become my partner on this?"

Jojo felt an electrical charge starting to zoom around inside her, so powerful that her knees were starting to shake. "Your partner?"

Jackson nodded, and Jojo had this sudden, bizarre impulse not just to shake his hand, but throw her arms around his neck. She was a pretty physical person who routinely gave hugs and cheek kisses. But this impulse was something else altogether. And with every second, the impulse grew stronger and stronger.

Jackson's palm still reached. "Maybe my problem lately is that I've been trying to do everything on my own. Maybe a partner will make the difference."

Jojo finally reached, too, and Jackson's fingers wrapped around hers. As the warmth traveled up Jojo's arm, giving her new courage, she couldn't control her joy. Her hands reached, her whole body moved toward him. As soon as her arms were around his neck, she knew that she'd been wanting to do that since the moment she'd walked in. Her cheek pressed against his. She felt feathery hair and warm skin. It was all so right, so perfect, that she almost burst into tears.

"Whoa," Jackson laughed as they finally broke apart and he regained his balance. "I guess that means yes." He looked down, a little embarrassed. "So I guess we're going to do this."

"I guess we will." Jojo stood, feeling as if she were going to float into the stratosphere. Even her smile felt different. Suddenly it was an unstoppable smile, as if every ounce of her body wanted to grin. She didn't come back down to earth until she caught sight of Miranda's activity report. How could she have forgotten? Miranda.

"Don't forget Miranda's activity report," she suddenly said, pointing to the paper. "I'll tell her I saw you. Okay?"

Jackson didn't react.

"Um, do you want me to give her a message?"

Jackson thought for a moment.

Jojo's heart stalled.

"No. No message," he finally said. "It's over between Miranda and me."

"It is?"

Jackson thought for a minute. "Yeah."

"That's too bad," Jojo sighed.

"Maybe," Jackson considered. "Maybe not."

He turned away and angrily swatted some papers off his desk.

Jojo stood watching him until she had the strong sense that he wanted to be alone again. "Anyway, I guess I'll find you again when I have some information."

"Sure," he said. "Or I'll find you."

"Okay."

"Talk to you soon." He smiled.

When Jojo was too self-conscious to stand there any longer, she backed out the door. She began jogging in the hall, then broke into a run down the stairs, finally leaping past the trophy case.

"Partners!" she cried, when she burst out into the parking lot. Maybe something was finally starting to happen, she realized as she broke into a full-speed run.

FIVE

Beep, bee, beep. Bee, bee, bee, beep.

"Miranda, it's Jojo. How was your honor society meeting? Good. I just called to tell you I dropped off your activity report at the newspaper office yesterday. I already told you? Oh . . . well, I just wanted to make sure. I know you still think about Jackson a lot, so I wanted you to know I hadn't forgotten. What? No. I don't mean anything. I'm going to help with something on the newspaper and I was just . . . oh, I don't know . . . never mind . . . forget I ever brought it up.

"You have to go? I bet you just need to write your welcome speech for the open house next weekend. I understand. Well, call me if you want to ride bikes or go to the beach or something. Or else I'll just see you on Monday. I guess I'll call Kat now. 'Bye."

Click.

Beep, bee, beep. Bee, bee, bee, beep.

"Hi, Mrs. McDonough. Kat's still at swim practice? I guess she must really want to win next week. No, it's not important. Just tell her I called. Everything's fine. Everything's great, actually. Thanks."

Click.

Beep, bee, beep. Bee, bee, bee, beep.

"Yo, Gabe. Of course it's Hernandez. No, I haven't talked to Kat. Actually, I just called her, but she wasn't home. No, she didn't say anything about a date with you, bozo breath.

"Anyway, I've just been thinking about something. Yes, it is amazing when I actually think. Anyway, I've been thinking about Chip taking all the blame after Brent pulled the fire alarm on Leanne. If I could just find someone else who actually saw Brent pull that alarm, I think I could straighten the whole thing out. And I'd really like to do that. More than anything. If you hear of anybody who might have actually seen Brent pull the alarm, will you let me know?

"Yeah. Leanne's here. At least I hope she's still here and that she didn't run down to the arcade or the amusement park. She just moved in. Chip brought her over after school, and she's still unpacking her stuff. She said she'd go to Kat's meet with us, too. But I don't want to ask about it right now. I'm trying not to bug her. My mom's serving dinner pretty soon, so I thought I'd give her a little space. . . ."

* * *

"Space," Leanne muttered, as every syllable from Jojo's phone calls poked through the wall that separated their bedrooms. Leanne had more space than if she were on the moon. Physical space, that is. The Hernandez house was three times the size of her mother's rented bungalow, and Jojo's sister's room was more than twice as big as Leanne's rented room downtown. Leanne even had her own bathroom, her own phone. But all of it — especially with Jojo's voice pushing through the pretty, pink wall — made Leanne feel as if she'd been squeezed into a shoe box.

Leanne threw herself across the frilly bed, unable to block out the sound as Jojo's voice bubbled up again.

"So, Gabe, maybe we should all go over to the Wave Cafe later tonight, like we always do. I'm sure Kat will just head over there after her practice. I don't know about Miranda. Okay. When I get off the phone, I'll ask Leanne. I'll tell her that Chip will be there, but if she wants to go down to the amusement park, I don't think I can stop her. Yeah. I'll talk to her as soon as we hang up. At least I'll try. I guess she's had enough time to get settled. We have to start talking to one another sometime. . . ."

* * *

"That's what you think," Leanne said, grabbing her patchwork velvet bag and pushing aside a little basket that Jojo had left, full of brand-new cosmetics, all in polite, pale peaches and pinks. Instead Leanne took her tin of rice powder, her red lipstick, and her near-empty coin purse.

She moved away from the sound of Jojo's voice. Leanne this, Leanne that. Let's solve Leanne's problems by finding her a place to live and letting everyone know that Brent pulled the fire alarm. Let's keep Leanne away from the low-life amusement park. Leanne will sit with us in the cafeteria, go to the swim meet, the Wave Cafe . . .

It was as if Leanne could suddenly be moved around and talked about. Maybe she was just a piece of property!

"So glad you all ask my opinion," Leanne muttered, as she heard Jojo say good-bye to Gabe and hang up the phone. "But this has nothing to do with me. It's all about what the rest of you want. Like I'm pet Leanne. Poor Leanne. First her mother's boyfriend hit her, so she had to move out. Then she got fired from her job, so she couldn't even afford to live on her own.

Gee, let's give her a place to live so we can all feel really superior."

Not waiting for Jojo to corner her, Leanne hurried out and headed for the backyard. She opened the sliding glass doors and stepped onto the patio around the pool. Soon her high heels were clattering along the driveway and into the street.

The minute Leanne turned onto Ocean Avenue, she started to feel like her own person again. The salty air soothed her, and the fog settled around her limbs. She kept running, pulling her ratty fur around her neck and leaving Jojo's tidy neighborhood behind. A few more blocks and she approached downtown. Over the Elk Creek Bridge and into the tourist district. Past the kite shop, the gift stores, the chowder restaurants, and the hot-dog stand shaped like a giant clam.

Leanne stopped at the end of Ocean Avenue, where it ran into the beach and intersected the promenade — the concrete walkway that bordered the sand. Fancy summer homes stretched out in one direction, topped by the new Tucker Resort. In the other direction was the old part of downtown. The pinball and video arcade. The pier. The amusement park, so run-down now that several rides had recently been condemned.

Leanne headed that way. She watched the lights twirl on the Ferris wheel. Even Chip didn't fit with this part of town. Her part of town. Leanne adored Chip. He was probably the first truly nice guy she'd ever known. But there was still so much that he didn't understand. He wanted her to fit in, to become one of them. He didn't understand that he was also asking her to throw away the person she'd always been. And if she did that, she would be admitting that the real Leanne Heard hadn't been worth anything.

Leanne crossed the pier and watched the water rumble and roll. As she strode closer to the amusement park, she focused on the lights, the twinkly music, and the smell of sugar crisps and cotton candy. Finally she just stood at the wire fence and watched the rides. The Big Thrill roller coaster. The Wild Ride, that looked like a cross between a huge hammer and a teeter-totter. The wooden boats that wobbled in and out of the old Tunnel of Love. Ron McGyver, the middle-aged park caretaker, took a break from the Wild Ride controls, stomped out a cigar, and waved to her. Leanne waved back to Ron and breathed a sigh of relief. Maybe the park was seedy and run-down. But at least it was real.

* * *

"Thanks for meeting me here."

"Of course. I'm glad you left a note for me. I'm happy to help."

"Well, help is what I need," Brent said.

Miranda smiled. "If you need more help, I brought my list of professionals in the area."

"Did you?"

"Phone numbers, too."

"I really appreciate that. But I'm counting on you. Let's find somewhere private."

"Fine. You lead the way."

Miranda followed Brent through the lobby of the Tucker Resort. She hadn't set foot in the place since the Turnaround Formal, when she'd left Eric and run off with Jackson. As she stepped past the guests in their leisure wear, she was amazed at how little she remembered about the resort. She'd blocked it out because of the pain that had followed. She'd made one brave move, only to wimp out later and let everything fall apart. Of course, the pain was behind her now. Now she was back to being the together, class president Miranda.

"Let's go upstairs," Brent said, leading her past the concierge desk and toward the elevator. He nodded at a bellhop, who practically bowed

back to him. "I don't want my father to find
us."

"Okay."

"You know how fathers are," Brent added.
"Mine isn't exactly interested in my problems."

Miranda nodded. Her own father expected so
much of her. Tonight he'd given her the third
degree after she'd gotten off the phone with Jojo,
before she'd slipped out of the house. She beat
Brent to the elevator and pushed the button.

Brent turned to face Miranda with his hands
on his hips. Then his eyes floated from her toes
to the top of her head and back again. "Here we
go."

Miranda ignored his leering. "Where are we
going?" she asked calmly.

"You'll see when we get there." Brent
winked. His golden hair flopped over one eye.
When the elevator finally arrived, he held the
door and ushered her in with a courtly gesture.

"Thank you." Miranda stepped into the corner and waited for the doors to close.

Brent followed her in.

She smiled again.

"I didn't want to talk to you at school," he
said, when the elevator began to climb. "This is
too . . . personal."

"I understand." Miranda looked out. One side of the elevator was made of glass and gave a view of the entire bay. "A Friends in Need peer counselor is supposed to go out of her way to help other students. I'm glad you contacted me."

His eyes were glued to her again, up and down her jeans, to her blazer, her long hair and back again. "Like the view?" he asked.

Miranda's smile wilted a little. She wasn't crazy about heights.

Still watching her, Brent fingered the elevator buttons. There was a slim gold ring on one hand, along with an expensive watch. "Anything I tell you is purely confidential, right?"

"Of course."

"Good. I want you to promise to keep it that way. I want to make sure that all our meetings will be kept a secret." He turned away to look at the elevator buttons. "Because of my father," he added.

The elevator slowed down, and Brent turned back. He was leaning back against the controls, his arms folded across his chest. For the longest time he just stood and stared at her.

Miranda took a deep breath. "So. You wanted to talk about Kat?" She knew she wasn't supposed to lead the counseling sessions, but she had to say something. She didn't know Brent at all. Most kids at school thought he was heaven, even though Kat, Gabe, and Chip said he was trouble. Kat had even suggested that Miranda back out of meeting Brent. And for once, Miranda didn't want to back out. She wanted to be bold. She wanted to face up.

"I'm not supposed to give advice, though," she added, remembering what she'd learned at her Friends in Need workshops. "I'm just supposed to listen."

"Okay," Brent said. "I'd like to talk about a lot of things."

"Like what?"

"Like school. Me. You," he answered.

Just then the elevator suddenly fell and jolted to a stop. Miranda gasped and almost stumbled. Brent reached out to catch her.

She caught her balance. "What just happened?"

"Nothing," he said, sticking close.

"But the elevator. It stopped."

He put his hands on her shoulders and grinned. "I stopped it. I just wanted to make sure we could be alone. You don't mind being alone with me. Do you?" He moved closer and one hand reached for her cheek.

Miranda's head began to throb. She felt the heat of his hand and tried to back away. But there was nowhere to back away to. "No. I don't mind . . . I just don't like heights very much."

He smoothed a wisp of hair off her face. "What's the matter? Are you scared? Should I call your daddy to come and get you?"

"No!" she reacted. "What does my father have to do with this?"

"I've been talking about my own father," Brent whispered. "If you have a thing about your father, that's your problem, not mine."

Miranda was starting to get dizzy. "Let's just leave me out of this."

"Why?" he challenged. "What are you afraid of?"

How could Brent have made her feel this way so quickly? She was afraid that she'd never have the guts to stand up to her father. That's what Jackson thought. Using all her courage, she stared back into Brent's blue eyes. "I'm not afraid of anything," she said.

"Well, I can tell that I've made you upset," Brent soothed, finally letting go of her and taking a step back. "Maybe we'd better finish this session for today and meet again when you're feeling better."

Part of Miranda knew that was a terrible idea, just as she'd known never to meet Brent alone in the first place. But she wanted to prove to him that he hadn't gotten to her. "I'm fine," she stuttered.

"Good." He smiled.

She reached for the elevator buttons, but he blocked her.

He had her pinned in the corner. "I didn't get very much counseling. I'd say you owe me another meeting, don't you think?"

She didn't answer.

"Or are you scared to meet me again?" he pouted. "Maybe you don't really want to help me. Or maybe you're afraid of what your daddy will think?"

Finally he moved away from her and reached for the emergency switch again. He pushed *On.* The elevator jolted, then began to move again. They rode in silence back down to the lobby.

When the doors opened again, Brent grabbed Miranda's arm. "I'll find you at school, or leave you another note. I know this hasn't been what you expected, but I need to see you again."

She stared right back at him. "All right," she managed.

He let her go as some tourists filed past to use

the elevator. "And I think you need me, too."

Miranda's body tensed as she stared back at him and realized that in some strange way he was right. The last time she'd been in this lobby was before she'd run off with Jackson. Maybe she needed to face the fact that it was over with Jackson. Maybe she needed to prove something to herself.

SIX

Monday morning, Chip slipped on his glasses, which hung from a cord around his neck. He and Gabe were tacking a banner in front of the guidance office that read CRESCENT BAY HIGH PARENT/TEACHER OPEN HOUSE. GET IN TOUCH AND STAY THERE. He gestured for Gabe to raise the banner's left side.

"I couldn't believe this weekend," Gabe said.

"Why? It was our crowd's normal, everyday weekend at the Wave Cafe," Chip replied, then he shook his head. "Gabe, the banner is crooked."

"Exactly."

"What?".

"That's exactly what I'm talking about," Gabe explained. "It was our same old normal weekend hanging out."

Chip pointed to the banner again.

Gabe took a running leap, then slapped the banner's sagging edge, as if he were making a jump shot.

"It's still crooked," Chip commented.

Gabe shrugged. "I just mean, after everything I said to Kat after our show last week, I couldn't believe we went right back to the same old hanging out with everybody at the Wave. Kat had to joke with all her friends from the swim team and do her funny monologues for everyone else in our class. I barely had five minutes alone with her."

Chip slipped his backpack off his shoulder. "At least Kat was there."

Gabe gave the banner one more tap. "But she didn't even mention our big date. I still don't know if she wants to go. She acted as if I'd never even asked her."

"Maybe she forgot."

"Right. Just like Leanne forgot to show up at the Wave at all."

Chip winced.

"Sorry," Gabe said, patting Chip's shoulder. "That was low. I'm really sorry."

"It's okay. You're right." Chip sighed. "I've asked Leanne to join us for ten things so far, and she hasn't shown up once. Jojo says Leanne doesn't even show up for meals at her house. Leanne must have to sneak sandwiches in the middle of the night, so she doesn't have to run into any of Jojo's family." Chip sat down with his back to the guidance office wall. He hugged his long legs and stared down at his sandals. "I don't know. Maybe I'm making too big a deal out of this."

Gabe flopped down next to him. "Maybe I have to make a bigger deal out of this date thing with Kat. We've been friends for so long, it's not that easy to switch gears. Maybe I should announce it on our next KHOT show." Gabe put on his radio deejay voice. "So, Patty Prom Queen, how about pretending it's prom time and saving the big dance for me? Just you and me — all alone." He looked at Chip, then groaned. "Ugh. Bad, huh?"

Chip pulled a thermos out of his pack. "Maybe I should try the opposite approach with Leanne — whatever that would be. Alone is usually okay with her and me. It's the minute any of my other friends are around that it all falls apart. Maybe I should just sit back and wait for her to get used to all of us."

Gabe nodded and took a swig of Chip's juice. "You know, maybe I will do something crazy for this date with Kat," he decided. "Not an announcement on our radio show, but something really public. Something Kat can't ignore no matter how hard she tries." He folded his hands over his black T-shirt. "You and Leanne still going to the meet the day after tomorrow?"

Chip nodded.

Gabe smiled. "Maybe I'll think of something by then."

Chip wished that he could think of something, too. He was usually so patient, but with Leanne his patience was running out. He was actually beginning to wonder if it was possible to have a relationship with Leanne without giving up his friends, the environmental club, and even his family. The only times he'd seen Leanne over the last week had been when absolutely no one else was around. They'd met once on the deserted soccer field, and taken a walk once after school to the old amusement park. There Leanne talked to some repair guy, a barker, and other amusement park people who had given Chip the creeps.

Chip could only pray that Kat's meet might make a difference. He was getting tired of being so sensitive and understanding. Sometimes he wondered if his niceness wasn't some huge KICK

ME sign, instructing all girls to treat him like dirt.

Finally the first-period bell went off, and both boys popped to their feet.

"By the way," Chip brought up, pointing to the crooked banner. "You going to go to this open house thing this weekend?"

Gabe nodded. "Kat and I are doing some KHOT routine. I don't know what. As usual, we'll make up half of it on the spot. I've been trying to plan our big date right afterwards. If she ever gives me a straight answer and tells me if she wants to go." He took a swig of Chip's juice, then handed the thermos back. "You going?"

"Hud is making me set up all the chairs," Chip replied. "That'll end my punishment for that stupid fight with Brent Tucker. At least I finally can put that mess behind me. Between you and me, though, I still think Tucker deserved a punch for what he did to Leanne."

Gabe started to join the hall traffic, then stopped, right in front of the student activity board. "Yo, Chip, that reminds me. Jojo wants to find another witness who saw Tucker pull that fire alarm. I think she wants to nail the guy."

"That's okay with me."

"Really." Gabe looked up and down the hall.

"And Simon Wheeler Dealer wanted to know if Jojo needed anything. Can you believe it? He has the hots for Hernandez. I said I'd help him out."

"Really?" said Chip.

Gabe nodded. "I'll just leave a note for him on the activity board. Maybe he can find another witness for Jojo."

Chip watched Gabe scribble a note to Simon, outlining Jojo's request. "Maybe I should leave a note for Leanne," he sighed. "Wanted. One public appearance. Just one."

Gabe stuck Simon's note onto the board. "Maybe I should leave one for Kat. One private appearance. And then a few more."

"NAH," they both said at the same time.

"See you," Chip said, parting from Gabe and heading for his biology class. He couldn't think of anything that would help his situation with Leanne anyway. And he sure couldn't imagine announcing his feelings for Leanne on the radio or giving her some big surprise at a swim meet. With Leanne, all he could do was wait. He just wondered how long his patience would hold out.

At the beginning of lunch period, Miranda led Kat and Jojo across the new, green quad. The three of them trudged in perfect step. First Miranda, in her jeans and shiny riding boots. Kat bounced after her, in baggy shorts, and plastic shoes that looked like giant gummy bears. Jojo brought up the rear, her curls neat, wearing very little makeup.

"Where are we going?" Jojo asked.

"I just want to check the activity board before you go to the cafeteria," Miranda told her. "Is that okay?"

"As long as it doesn't take too long," Kat offered. "I'm starving."

Miranda slowed for a moment and pulled a sandwich out of her briefcase. She handed it to Kat. "Here, I'm not hungry."

Kat grabbed it. "Feed me and I'll follow you anywhere." She made a muscle. "Since I've been in training, my metabolism is on warp nine."

They stepped over other students as they crossed the grass, avoiding sunbathers, open notebooks, and a fierce Frisbee game.

"Want some, Jo?" Kat offered a bite of Miranda's sandwich to Jojo as they ducked back into the covered corridor.

Jojo shook her head. "No, thanks. I don't mind waiting till we get back to the caf."

Kat kept chowing down. "Actually, I

wouldn't mind avoiding the cafeteria completely today," Kat said. "Every time I run into Gabe now, he stares at me like I have something hanging from my nose. It makes me feel so . . . so . . ."

"So what?" Jojo asked.

"I don't know!" Kat shook her head and stomped her feet. "I don't want to think about him until my meet is over! I don't want to deal with this!"

Jojo patted her as they passed the library, which was covered with posters advertising History Week. Miranda led them around a corner, past the guidance office, until they reached the glass-covered activity board. The three of them stopped to stare. Lists and brochures had been pinned under the glass, with a few notes taped to the outside.

Kat pointed. "Hey, look. There's a note for Wheeler Dealer. You didn't leave that, did you, Jo?"

At first Jojo wasn't even sure what Kat was talking about. Then she saw Simon's name on the folded piece of paper. "Why would I leave a note for Simon Wheeldon?" she asked. Just because she and Simon had sold ads together for the talent show program was no reason to think she'd leave notes for him. She hadn't given him two seconds' thought since then.

Meanwhile Miranda was staring intently at the Friends in Need section.

"Are you expecting a note?" Jojo asked her, remembering that she'd overheard Miranda and Kat talking about Brent at her home.

Miranda looked a little alarmed, then shook her head. "No. Nothing."

Jojo wasn't sure what else to say. She hadn't told anyone about overhearing the conversation about Brent, and she didn't intend to. Maybe she used to blab secrets to the entire school, but no more. She was the new Jojo now, and she had important things to do.

Suddenly something crazy was going on inside Jojo, and she wasn't sure why. Her heart had just started beating at hyper-speed, and her skin felt hot. It took her a moment to even realize what had triggered her feelings. Jackson was trotting silently toward them, his skateboard almost hidden under his leather jacket.

Miranda stiffened and blushed.

Jackson's face was flushed, too, and he was a little out of breath. As he jogged closer, he dropped his skateboard and with a daring look toward the principal's office, glided up to them.

The wheels sounded like a toy train as they scraped the linoleum floor. As soon as Jackson reached them, he jumped off the board, flipped it with his foot, and stowed it.

"That was daring," Miranda snapped.

Jackson stared at her. "I wasn't trying to be daring. I'm just in a hurry."

Miranda took a step toward him. "So why don't you ride your skateboard right into the principal's office?"

"Maybe I will," Jackson replied.

"Well . . . go ahead," Miranda shot back.

Jojo took a step back, leaving a clear path for Jackson and Miranda to glare at each other. She turned toward the guidance office, so she wouldn't have to feel the current that always crackled between them. But then, to her amazement, Jackson walked right past Miranda and tapped her arm instead.

"Jojo, can I talk to you for a second?" Jackson panted, giving Miranda only the slightest second glance.

"You want to talk to me?" Jojo's heart thudded in her chest.

He nodded.

Now it was Miranda who moved out of the way. She quickly took her things-to-do calendar out of her briefcase and moved close to the board, checking it as if she had twelve appointments that afternoon. At the same time, Kat dug through Miranda's briefcase, searching for more food.

Jojo joined Jackson in a private little niche between the guidance and attendance offices. "What is it?" she whispered. Her heart was still pounding away.

He smiled and took a deep breath. "Hi, partner."

"Hi."

"Any progress?"

Jojo began chattering. Otherwise, she might have melted on the floor. "No. Not yet. I haven't found out anything about Brent yet. I've talked to a few people, but nobody knows anything about the fire alarm. I won't give up, though. I promise I won't."

"I know you won't." He glanced back once at Miranda, then focused on Jojo again. "I didn't expect anything so soon, anyway. If we do get a story, I figured it wouldn't be until the next issue."

Jojo focused on his brilliant eyes. "Okay."

He shifted his skateboard, balancing a stack of papers under his other arm. "But I had a last-

minute idea for this issue, the one that goes to
the printer's this afternoon, so we can get it out
by Wednesday. I wanted to know if you really
meant it when you said you didn't care if I threw
out the cheerleading photo."

"Of course I meant it," Jojo breathed.

He brushed sweat off his forehead. "Okay.
Because I wrote a new cover piece. It's about
some of the things you told me last week. Don't
worry, I didn't use Leanne's name or make it so
that anyone could identify her. I just felt inspired
by what you did."

"By me?" Jojo thought about Leanne. If
Leanne knew that she was the inspiration for a
newspaper article, she'd never speak to Jojo
again.

Jackson touched her shoulder. "I couldn't stop
thinking about it. All weekend I kept thinking
about how brave you are, and how chicken I've
been with this issue of the paper. Anyway, I just
wanted to make sure you didn't mind."

Jojo thought about Leanne again. But then
Jackson took a step closer and thoughts of anyone else flew out of her head. "I don't mind."

"Great." Jackson set down his skateboard
again. "I've got to get to the journalism room.
We can talk again soon. As soon as you find an

eyewitness, find me and let me know."

Jojo prayed that a witness would somehow magically show up. She tried to think of anyone else who might have seen Brent pull that stupid alarm. "I will. You know I will."

"I know." Then the metal skateboard wheels clattered against the floor again, and Jackson was off, just missing the principal who stuck his head out and frowned.

Jojo stared after Jackson, her heart still on overdrive. She was wearing that whole body smile again and clutching her arms as if it would make her feel the pressure of his hands again.

That was when Miranda slowly walked up behind her. She tapped her schedule book with her pencil and bit her lip.

"What did he want?" Miranda asked.

Jojo bit her lip. "Something for the paper."

Kat joined them, too. "What was that about?" she chimed in.

Before Jojo could give a more detailed answer, Miranda raised a hand and insisted, "Never mind! I don't care. It doesn't matter to me. Don't even tell me."

"Why?" Jojo asked.

"Because I thought about him all weekend," Miranda said.

"You did?" Jojo asked breathlessly. Her heart flopped back into the pit of her stomach.

"Never think about some guy all weekend," Kat teased. "It rots your brain."

Miranda didn't laugh. "That's not what I meant." She put her calendar back into her briefcase. "I thought about how wrong I was to try and keep our relationship going. I thought about how it's all over between him and me."

"Are you sure?" Jojo gasped.

"It has to be over," Miranda promised. "It is."

Kat put her arm around Miranda. They began to walk, but Jojo hung back. They didn't even notice that Jojo hadn't kept up with them, but for once Jojo didn't let that bother her. She was too carried away by the incredible feeling she had inside.

SEVEN

With the exception of the swim team athletes, Simon Wheeldon was the first to arrive at the Crescent Bay public pool. His last-period class was Practical Business Skills, which usually meant leaving campus to interview some lawyer or doing a two-week internship at the Burger Barn. What it also meant was that nothing much happened in the classroom, so Simon had a lot of opportunities to leave school early.

He sat alone on the concrete in his western shirt and crisp jeans, a few feet outside the pool's front door. Dwarfed by the team bus from Crestview, he ignored the smell of chlorine that wafted out every time some swimmer tramped in or out from the indoor pool.

Simon pulled a neat stack of paperwork out of his zippered pouch and started to sort through it. He had homework questions for government class . . . new vocabulary words for Spanish. But he put those aside to reflect on his most important piece of paper. His note from Gabe.

Simon read it over for about the tenth time.

> *Yo Dealdon — What does la Jojo want? Okay. She wants firsthand dirt on Brent Tucker. Remember that alarm that went off in the middle of Leanne Heard's talent show song? Jo wants an eye witness to the event, one willing to testify. Don't know why. Can't begin to guess. Good luck, dude.*
>
> *P.S. That CD is the best.*

Simon folded up the note again, lifted his string tie, and stuck the note into his shirt pocket. He wasn't sure why he liked Jojo so much. He didn't hang out with her crowd. He didn't hang out with any crowd. He and Jojo hadn't even gotten along when they'd sold ads together. But who knew why anyone fell for someone else. He just knew that he liked Jojo's dark eyes and perfect smile. He liked that searching expression on her face and her energetic, petite frame.

Maybe he just liked the way she smelled.

Simon was trying to remember the exact way

that Jojo smelled — sort of like powder and trees — when another much less pleasant scent overpowered him. This smell was so strong that at first Simon thought it was the chlorine again. But then he heard two sets of footsteps and realized that it was a double dose of perfume.

A moment later, two female voices replaced the sound of footsteps. The girls had stopped on the other side of the Crestview bus. Simon could only see their shadows peeking out around the bumper.

"Brandy, I'm telling you, Brent is up to something."

"Come on, Lisa. Just because Brent came up to talk to me in the cafeteria, why does that have to mean he's up to anything?"

"Because he didn't come up to talk to you, Brandy. He came up to talk to me."

"Oh, really?"

"Brandy."

"God, Lisa. I'm starting to get sick of this. Did you ever stop to think that maybe every guy who comes within five miles of us isn't totally obsessed with *you*?"

"Brandy, get real."

Simon identified the voices' owners long before the girls sauntered around the side of the bus and stood in front of him. Brandy Kurtz was in her cheerleading uniform, clutching two pairs of pompoms. She had red and white ribbons in her hair and was certainly there early because of her duties as head cheerleader. Lisa Avery, wearing a unitard and smearing on another coat of lip gloss, had probably just cut class.

Brandy practiced a little leap, not even noticing that she'd landed on Simon's notebook. Both girls acted as if he were part of the concrete, which was pretty much what Simon had expected. Girls like Brandy and Lisa never paid much attention to guys like him.

"When is this meet supposed to start, anyway?" Lisa asked Brandy.

"The spirit bus should arrive any minute," Brandy sighed. "You know, you didn't have to come early with me if you didn't want to."

"Anything's better than typing class." Lisa rolled her eyes. "I just wish *someone* would get here."

Simon tried not to feel offended. But it was hard just to sit there while two great-looking girls acted as if he were a worm who'd crawled out of the pool dressing room. Trying to appear busy, he took the next sheet of paper and unfolded it in his lap. It was the brand-new issue of *Bay News*, hot off the press. Simon had picked up one of the first copies from the journalism room on his way off campus.

Simon hadn't even begun to skim the article on the front page when a shadow suddenly blocked his light. The perfume smell grew stronger. When Simon glanced up, he saw Brandy looming over him, while Lisa posed a few feet away. She was picking at her nail polish.

"Can I see that?" Brandy demanded, reaching down for Simon's newspaper.

Simon held on to it.

"We were supposed to be on the front page!" Brandy cried to Lisa. "You know Sarah what's-her-face, who takes pictures for the paper?"

Lisa shrugged.

"Well, I had to practically break her arm to get her to take another picture of the squad," Brandy raved. "She finally did, and she promised me it was going to be on the front page of this issue."

"So?" Lisa said.

"So look." Brandy pulled Lisa over to read Simon's paper. "There's no picture on the front page at all. Just some article called . . ." She bent

over and squinted. "It's something by that
weird — but cute — Jackson Magruder called
'Taking a Chance.' "

"Maybe it's a secret letter to Miranda Jamison," Lisa quipped. "Talk about taking a chance.
Maybe someone dared Jackson to fall for her. If
you ask me, that's the only way I could see some
guy going for her. She's probably as much fun
as a final exam."

"They're not even together anymore,"
Brandy whined.

"Good," Lisa said, smiling. "It's about time
someone figured out that she's a fake. Little Miss
Perfect, president of this, queen of that . . ."

"Lisa, shut up. I want to read this."

Lisa huffed.

Simon read, too, while Brandy hunkered over
him.

> *Taking a chance.*
>
> *A cheerleader notices a homeless girl, a
> girl that no one else in school has time for.
> This cheerleader is popular. What can the
> homeless girl do for her? Nothing. But the
> cheerleader asks her to move in with her
> and her family.*
>
> *She takes a chance.*

Meanwhile, the rest of us just plod along, stuck in our ruts and afraid to take any kind of risk. . . .

Simon kept reading, drawn in by Jackson's article. Suddenly it all came together in his head. He remembered Jojo mentioning that she was friends with a girl who'd had to leave her mother's house. Jojo had wanted to help her, and now she'd actually done it.

"Jojo!" Simon said out loud. "Good for you!"

"Is this about Jojo?" Brandy gasped.

Simon glanced up.

"What about Jojo?" Lisa intruded.

"This article is about Jojo Hernandez," Brandy realized. "What other cheerleader would do something like that? And I bet that homeless girl is that creepy Leanne Heard," Brandy snapped. "Leanne deserves to be on the street. She never talks to anyone. She just gives me looks like I deserve to be shot or something."

"I know," said Lisa.

"If you ask me," Brandy went on, "Leanne deserved it when Brent pulled the fire alarm during the talent show. When we saw him do it I almost applauded. And I was so glad he didn't get blamed."

Lisa frowned.

Simon's mouth fell open. "WHAT?"

Brandy ignored him. "Maybe I should just let everyone in school know who this article is really about. Maybe then I could get Jojo kicked off the squad or something."

"I wouldn't count on anything," Lisa said as she joined Brandy over the newspaper. "If people know this article is really about Jojo, they might want to nominate her for sainthood or something. Forget Jojo. We have to keep thinking about Brent."

"Brent? What about him?" Brandy argued. "Lisa, just because he's only the most gorgeous guy in this school, and I have a crush on him, doesn't mean you have to put him down. You know, sometimes a guy does look at someone besides you."

"I wouldn't get my hopes up about Brent if I were you," Lisa warned.

"Why not?"

"That's a stupid question, Brandy. Just turn around and you'll see why not."

Simon's head was spinning so fast already, just trying to follow Lisa and Brandy's conversation, that he turned and looked, too. The Crescent Bay High spirit bus had chugged into the pool parking lot. Plastered on one side was a poster that read, KAT IS TOO HOT TO LOSE. IT'S TOTALLY IMPOSSIBLE, in huge neon letters. And below the poster, students were already filtering off the bus, heading toward the pool.

"Open your eyes and look," Lisa insinuated.

Brandy craned her neck, and Simon glanced over at the same time. Miranda Jamison was striding away from the bus, hugging her briefcase as if it were a shield, while Brent Tucker trotted behind her. When he caught up, he blocked her path and whispered something into her ear. She tensed and sped up, almost as if she were running away from him. Brent chuckled to himself and continued to trail her across the blacktop.

"I knew it!" Lisa gasped. "I knew there was something going on with Brent and Miranda."

Then Jojo bounced off the bus, followed by Gabe and Chip. Simon's head swam as he watched her. All of it was so confusing that for a few moments Simon's business head had almost gone completely down the drain.

"Wait a minute," Simon managed, when he realized that Brandy and Lisa were wandering away from him. Brandy was gathering the other cheerleaders, while Lisa ran up to Eric Geraci,

snaked herself around him, and kissed her way
up his neck.

It took a moment for Simon to think back and
realize what had just happened. He'd found what
Jojo was looking for. Brandy and Lisa knew
about Brent and the fire alarm!

"Brandy!" he called.

Brandy wouldn't turn around.

"Lisa!" he yelled.

Lisa glanced back and glared, then nibbled at
Eric's ear.

Okay. Simon would find a better time. He
probably needed some time to think and plan.
Just getting those girls to talk to him again would
be a feat. Simon was not a football captain or
frat brat.

But one thing that Simon did know was that
he was clever. He was persistent. And he could
always offer Brandy and Lisa something irre-
sistible in exchange.

Miranda's head felt fuzzy — or maybe it was
just the humid air. Her thoughts were confused — or maybe it was just the sound echoing
off the tile walls. She tried to concentrate on the
shrill whistles and the slap of the water as the
swimmers dove and splashed, but all she could

think about was Jackson and Brent.

"When did you say Kat's race was?" she asked Gabe and Chip in a distracted voice.

Chip didn't answer.

"After the backstroke," Gabe answered brightly.

"Thanks."

The three of them were sitting together, to form a "united wall of cheering" for Kat. But they were acting as separate as if they were watching three different sporting events. Gabe was finishing some kind of spirit banner he planned to hang in time for Kat's race. The painted bed sheet was wadded up on the bleacher seat beside him. He took little circles of paper and wrote *KHOT always wins* on them in neon-yellow ink, then pinned them to the edges of the sheet.

Meanwhile, Chip cleaned his glasses with his Sierra Club sweatshirt. After putting them on, he turned away from the competition in the water and watched the pool entrance. As each latecomer straggled in, he leaned forward, only to sigh with disappointment and sit back again.

"I'm going to wait until the last second before Kat's event," Gabe said as he fastened on more KHOT circles.

Chip shook his head. "I should have known she would never show up. . . ."

"See, I did this in stages. First the sign on the side of the bus . . ." Gabe explained.

"Maybe I knew all along that she wouldn't really come through," Chip continued.

"Then the KHOT stickers I put up in the foyer . . ."

"Maybe I was a fool to have ever fallen for her."

"This will be the final kicker. This will make her win for sure, and realize that I'm serious. Just when Kat is ready for her race, I'm going to unroll this. . . ."

Chip nodded, even though he hadn't heard Gabe at all. "It's just so great when it's just us and nobody else is around."

"Then there will be no looking back." Gabe stood up. "Come on, Chip. Will you help me put this up?"

Chip nodded, even though he didn't seem to have heard Gabe at all. "I don't know what to do."

Miranda didn't know what to do, either. Ever since her "counseling session" with Brent that previous weekend, she'd been feeling woozy. Unstable. The feeling had gotten stronger when she'd run into Jackson in the hall. Standing there with Kat and Jojo, she'd wanted to say, Stop, time out. She'd wanted to sit down with Jackson and say, Now that we're finally talking, why are we fighting with each other? But she hadn't been able to do that, so she'd lashed out, then retreated while Jojo tried to cover up for her.

By the time Brent had followed her off the spirit bus, "just to say hello," she was almost dizzy. And she didn't feel any stronger now that the meet was in full swing. Her head was light. Her stomach kept flipping over. And it wasn't from the humidity or the chlorine. No. This was the same feeling she'd had before she'd run off with Jackson. It made her feel that nothing in her well-planned life made sense. If she didn't do something crazy, even something wild, she was going to smother under all of her good grades and marks of success.

Miranda pulled her blazer more tightly around herself. She tried to focus her mind again by remembering her dates for her upcoming history test. She shifted, stretched her legs, and tried to watch the swimmers slicing across the pool.

"Miranda," Gabe suddenly called, "can you hand me that roll of tape I brought? It's under my notebook. Under my copy of *Bay News*."

Miranda glanced at Gabe's newspaper and handed the tape up to him. She quickly sat back down because she was no longer able to stand. The sight of Jackson's article on the front page of the paper had made her feel as if she were going to tumble down into the pool. Gabe and Chip hadn't read the new issue yet, but she'd picked up an early copy in the student government room. She'd read it over on the spirit bus. She knew that Jackson's story wasn't just about Jojo and Leanne. The article was also about her.

The rest of us just plod along, stuck in our ruts and afraid to take any kind of risk.

The words were plastered on the inside of Miranda's forehead. She couldn't stop thinking about them until she suddenly felt something come up from underneath the bleachers and brush against her ankle. At first she thought it was that feeling again. She was getting so woozy that she was going to slip down under the bleachers. But then she reached down to push whatever it was away and she saw a hand. A boy's hand reached up through the wooden slats and wrapped itself around her leg.

Miranda gasped. For some reason she still

thought of Jackson. Not that Jackson would do something like that, but she'd seen him at the meet earlier. He'd been wandering around, probably looking for the best place to watch the races for his newspaper work. Jackson was the only person she knew quirky enough to watch swimming from underneath the seats.

When she reached down, another hand reached up from under the bleacher and clasped hers. She managed to stay on the bench, slightly stooped over. She looked to Gabe and Chip, but they were both busy hanging Gabe's sheet from the top of the bleachers. She looked for Jojo, but she was still down near the other cheerleaders. Finally Miranda dared to look down between the slats of the bleachers.

"Hi."

"It's you."

"You're right. It's me." Brent's brilliant blue eyes peered up at her.

The air seemed thicker than ever. He held her hand so tightly that her fingers stung. "You scared me."

"You scare awfully easily," he said.

She wrenched her fingers out of his grasp.

He kept his other hand on her calf.

"What are you doing?"

"Nothing. Just trying to get your attention."

"You have my attention. What do you want?" She stared down at his golden hair through the wooden slats.

"I have to talk to you again," he said, refusing to let go of her leg. "Meeting at the resort was a mistake. I don't want to go anywhere where we could possibly run into my dad."

Miranda didn't want to meet him again. She didn't want to be locked in some elevator, or attacked from under a bench. She didn't want to look in Brent's blue eyes and see a tiny reflection of her own confusion and doubt.

"How about Friday night?" he suggested.

"That's the open house," she said, relieved to have an excuse. "I have to make the welcome speech at seven-thirty."

He undid the buckle on her shoe, then stroked her foot. "So, meet me at six, and I'll have you back at school in time. I don't know where yet. I'll leave you a note on the activity board."

She tried to squirm away from him.

"Unless you're afraid to meet me again," he whispered.

Miranda glanced down at the pool again, hoping to see Kat. Maybe the sight of strong, funny Kat in her red-and-white Speedo would make her feel more secure. Instead, she spotted Jackson, who was chatting with the coach on the bottom bleacher. As if he'd felt her looking at him, Jackson suddenly raised his head. Just as their eyes met, Brent reached up to grab her hand again. She lurched forward, almost falling off the bleacher bench.

"All right," Miranda told Brent as he squeezed her fingers.

"Will you meet me? I need you, Miranda. I need to talk to you again."

"Fine," Miranda said, staring down at Jackson again. "Whatever you want. I'll meet you on Friday night."

Brent caressed her ankle, then finally let her go.

Miranda was so dizzy that she could barely see. She knew she was destined to take Brent up on his dare, even if it meant getting dragged down to his level.

EIGHT

"*We have the results of the girls' backstroke. First place with a new district record is Carrie McGraw from Crestview High. Placing second, from Crescent Bay High, is Maria Bononi. And third place, also from Crescent Bay High, is freshman Patricia Slover. Congratulations to you all!*"

"*YAAAAAAAAAAAYYYYYY!!*"

Jackson tried to block out all the background noise. The splashing. The echoey rumble. The starting guns, announcements, and cheers.

"Inspiration," he whispered as he sat on the bottom bleacher. He was straining to keep his eyes on his notepad and not stare up at Miranda. "Not distraction," he reminded himself. "Inspiration."

At least Jojo had finally inspired him to bring *Bay News* back from the dead. He'd written his

"Taking a Chance" article in one sleepless night, then gotten last-minute approval to print it.

And now I'm watching this swim meet, he wrote in his notepad, *as if it were just . . . a swim meet.*

For Jackson, a swim meet should just be the jumping off point. From there he could explore why the pool water was that particular color of blue. Who made the coaches' whistles. He could even explore why the most beautiful part was the gymnastic underwater turns that the swimmers made between laps.

So far that day he was a big blank. He'd tried every trick to spark his imagination. He'd quizzed the woman who managed the pool. He'd stopped to just smell the chlorine and feel the heavy air. He'd managed to get the coach to chatter on about the psychology of competing, which might have led to something interesting. But then he'd seen Miranda on the top bleacher just as she'd lurched forward on the bench, as if she'd dropped her only copy of a term paper through the slats of the bleacher floor. After that, any spark of inspiration had flown out of Jackson's head.

"Come on," he told himself. "Look. Listen. Think." Then he sighed and glanced up to the top of the bleachers again.

Miranda looked truly upset. Her usually perfect posture looked strained and her long hair looked sloppy. Something about her face worried him, but Jackson told himself not to do anything. Miranda had probably just lost some homework or a brochure for some fancy college. She didn't need his help. She didn't want his help! She'd made it so obvious when he ran into her at the activity board that she regretted ever having gotten involved with him. She probably agreed with her father now, that Jackson was a huge mistake.

Don't think about this, he jotted down. *Think about your story. Let go! Free write. Think!*

Desperate to jump start his brain, Jackson began to stroll. Running his hands along the frame of the temporary bleachers, he walked up the concrete ramp toward the exit. The benches rose alongside him. When he finally reached the last bleacher, he swung on one of the supporting metal posts, stretching his arm and letting out a tiny groan.

That was when Jackson saw him. He froze, surprised to spot anyone in the semidarkness beneath the stands. The boy moved easily, as if he'd memorized the place. After a moment,

Jackson recognized Brent Tucker. Brent ducked out, wiping his hands. He blinked, adjusting to the bright pool area lights.

"Hey, Tucker," Jackson said, standing right in Brent's path. "What's under there?"

"Excuse me," Brent answered, barely looking at Jackson.

Jackson didn't move. "What are you doing?"

Brent didn't seem to have another answer. And he didn't need one because just then two senior jocks hung down from the bleacher to affectionately swat him with their Crescent Bay High baseball caps.

"Come on up here, Tucker."

"Where you been, Brent?"

"We have to talk to you, Tucker. Get up here!"

"Hey, guys," Brent called back. He glanced up to where Miranda was sitting, then grabbed one of the caps and stuck it on his head. "I'm on my way."

Before Brent could trot up to join his buddies, Jackson grabbed Brent's arm. For some reason his body was suddenly surging with rage. His heart was pumping, his mouth had gone dry, and he wasn't quite sure why.

"You didn't answer me, Brent," Jackson insisted, pointing under the stand. "What were you doing under there?"

Brent just grinned and his blue eyes drifted up to where Miranda was sitting again. Then he punched Jackson's arm with a super-familiar, almost dirty laugh. A moment later, Brent had jogged down to the bottom of the bleachers, then leaped up to join the jocks.

Jackson reacted as if he'd just been knocked over. All Jackson really knew about Brent was that he was rich and smooth. But something about Brent had always bothered him, and now he felt as if his body had been filled with molten lead. He'd known that he wasn't really over Miranda, but he'd still prided himself on being cool and objective. Not anymore. Now he felt like running up the bleachers and throwing Brent Tucker down into the pool.

But of course Jackson didn't do anything. He just stood seething while Brent and his buddies laughed; the next race began, and Miranda stared down at the water. Jackson was staring so hard, trying to wipe out the insane anger inside his head, that he didn't see the sweet-faced girl jogging up the aisle until she'd stopped a few feet away from him.

"Hi," she said in a soft voice.

It took a moment for Jackson to register just who it was. With her red-and-white jumper, she could have been anyone on the drill team, the cheer squad, or the Pep Club. But as her pom-poms continued to rattle, Jackson realized that it was Jojo.

Of course. Jojo.

"Are you all right?" she asked.

He wasn't sure what to say. He wanted to drag Brent Tucker off the bleachers and tear him apart, but other than that he was the normal, reasonable Jackson. "I'm fine," he said.

"Oh." She still looked concerned. She started to take a step toward him, then stopped and smiled. "Okay."

They watched the water for a while. The butterfly race ended, and it was time for the girls' individual freestyle. There were several *splish, splash, splash* sounds as the swimmers jumped into the water for their pre-race dip.

"Have you found out anything about Brent yet?" he asked Jojo.

She looked down at her shoes. "Not yet. I've been trying, though."

"I know you have." He tried to think about his paper again, but his brain was still filled with

Miranda and Brent. "Let me know as soon as you find out anything. Call me anytime. I want you to come to the newspaper office whenever you can."

She tipped her face up to his. "Okay."

"I don't know what I'd do if you hadn't come along," he admitted.

Jojo shrugged. "Really?"

Jackson allowed himself one more glance up at Miranda. "Jojo, we have to get this story. I want to do whatever I have to do to nail Brent Tucker."

"Is that all you want?" Jojo asked in a breathless voice.

He finally looked at her alert brown eyes and determined little mouth. He wasn't sure why some people had ever referred to Jojo as superficial. He saw a girl who was as intense and passionate as anyone on his newspaper staff.

When Jackson didn't say anything else, Jojo made a move to rejoin the other cheerleaders. "I guess I'll go back," she said. "I don't want to bug you. I'll leave you alone."

He reached for her without even thinking. "Don't go," he said, his hand on her shoulder.

"Why?"

"I need you."

"You do?"

"We need to nail Brent Tucker, no matter
what it takes. I want to follow him, I want to
know everything he's been doing and see if
there's anything else you and I should know
about."

Jojo gazed at him, her eyes glued to his.
"Okay, partner."

Jackson didn't want to shake hands this time.
He was still too angry for a mere business gesture. He'd liked the way Jojo had just hugged
him in the newspaper office, as if hugging were
the normal way to start a partnership. He
thought that showed openness on Jojo's part.
Intensity. Qualities that made a good reporter.

Wanting to be as free as Jojo, he grabbed her
by her slender shoulders and pulled her to him.
As his arms wove around her, she moved in to
him so quickly, so tightly, that he wasn't sure
how to react.

"We've got to do this, Jojo," he promised.

"Okay," she answered in a shaky voice. "You
can count on me."

Kat was ready.
She shook out her arms, throwing drops of
water onto the concrete. Then she stepped up

on the starting block and did arm circles for her final warmup. She adjusted her goggles and her cap. She tugged at her suit. She crouched and breathed deeply, feeling that perfect combination of excitement and relaxation.

Watch my wake, she thought, not bothering even to look at her competition. She didn't care about any of them. This was a race against time. A race for her own personal best. Take a deep breath and go, go, go.

She could barely wait for the race to begin.

It had been so long since she'd felt this centered. Since swim season a year ago, before she'd had that painful romance last summer. Before she'd met Brent. Before she flipped over one hundred and eighty degrees in her feelings for Gabe.

"THHHHHHHAEEEEEE!!!!!!!!" shrieked a coach's whistle.

Kat got on her mark.

"RELAX. Take a minute before the race girls," one of the coaches announced. "We need to get something out of the water."

Sighing in disappointment, Kat stepped off the block. She pushed up her goggles, glancing up enough to see the coaches fishing out some green balloons — certainly thrown in by Crestview fans. One balloon evaded the coach's net, and a swimmer had to go in after it. Knowing that she had another minute to kill, Kat finally raised her eyes to take in the stands.

There was a good crowd. Kat spotted Jojo right away, sitting with the cheerleaders and wearing a dreamy smile. She scanned up the bleachers looking for Miranda. But before she found her best friend, her eyes were assaulted with neon so eye-popping it made the glistening blue water look drab.

NUMBER-ONE DUDETTE! MCDONOUGH IS HOT. AFTER THIS FRIDAY NIGHT THERE'LL BE NO TURNING BACK. IT'S US IN FIRST PLACE.

Gabe, what are you doing? Kat wanted to scream. She'd managed to ignore the KHOT buttons in the foyer and the gossip about Gabe's poster on the bus. She hadn't wanted to think about those things, because they put so much pressure on her.

Maybe the big date was the same way. That was an awful lot of pressure, too. After being the kinds of buddies who hung out in one another's bedrooms, Kat couldn't imagine suddenly putting on pantyhose and mascara for some nerve-wracking date. Where would they go? Gabe didn't have money for some fancy dinner and, even though she didn't live in a trailer park, her family wasn't exactly rolling in dough. Neither of them had a car. What was it going to be? Gabe's mother dropping them off in her 1972 Dodge Dart? And what if they had a terrible time? What if they set up this BIG DATE that was supposed to change their relationship for good, and it turned out to be nothing but a BIG DUD?

"ON YOUR MARKS!"

"What?" Kat muttered. She suddenly looked around as if she didn't quite know where she was. Then she saw the other girls settled onto their blocks and get into starting position. Off balance, she clambered up, too.

Crackkkkkkkkkkkkkk!

It wasn't until the starting gun echoed off the walls that Kat realized how much she'd let herself get distracted. Arms up, she told herself. Legs together. Head down.

Go!

But as soon as she hit the water, she knew that she'd blown it. Her legs kicked separately from her torso. Her arms flailed. She swallowed water, and her side stung from her badly executed dive. When she finished her first lap, she misjudged her turn so badly that she had to back up and tap the wall just so that she wouldn't be disqualified.

Nonetheless, she didn't give up. She tried to make up time. She counted her breaths. She concentrated on the economy of her stroke. She kept trying, even though she felt as if she were scooping through mud, and her lungs screamed for air. She managed to catch up to the pack by the beginning of the third lap.

By the last lap, she was finally back in form. In, two three, out, two three. Stroke, kick, head turn, breath. She wasn't sure exactly where the other swimmers were, but she knew that she wasn't far behind.

When her hand slammed into the side of the pool, she was still trying, still working with every last bit of energy and will. She whipped off her goggles and pushed up the flaps of her cap.

It only took Kat a second to figure out where she'd placed. She was angry. She was frustrated. All she'd wanted from the afternoon was to swim a decent race. And, thanks to Gabe — thanks to herself — she'd come in dead last.

NINE

The swim meet might have been over, but Leanne wasn't done. She was tearing her new bedroom apart. She'd taken the posters off the walls, the dust ruffle off the bed. She'd tossed out the makeup, comedy tapes, and magazines. She'd thrown the books labeled *Return this book to Miranda Jamison* into a heap on the closet floor.

The whole Hernandez house gave Leanne the spooks. The thick carpet, air conditioning, subdued lighting. Jojo's sister's bed was a prissy thing with four posts and a canopy. The bedroom was filled with so much frill and froufrou that it made Leanne want to scream.

"I hate you all!" Leanne cried out.

She really wanted to yell now that she knew Jojo was about as frilly as a boa constrictor. Leanne should have expected it. She'd never wanted this "friendship" with Jojo. She'd certainly never asked for it. She'd always known that girls like Jojo would only backstab and betray her.

Still rifling through the closet, Leanne considered gathering her few ragged things and moving out. Sure, she had no money. No job. But she would figure out something. She'd gotten by before.

"But where are my clothes?" she whispered as she sorted through the things left behind by Jojo's sister. She tore down hangers, pawed through drawers. Where was all her stuff? Her thrift-store finds, so painstakingly hunted out and purchased for a dollar or two, were gone!

Leanne had brought her entire wardrobe in a pillowcase. No suitcases or steamer trunks for her. Nothing but the kind of Goodwill style that she'd gotten used to on her own. But even her pillowcase had disappeared. Leanne searched more furiously, flinging out the hand-me-down sweaters and shoes until she heard someone outside the door.

"Oh, great," she muttered.

She tried not to move, not to breathe. Jojo's parents had gone to some society doctor party. They hadn't said when they were going to get back. Leanne had no desire to make chitchat with the eternally cheerful Mrs. Hernandez.

"Knock . . . knock," said a soft, tentative voice. "Leanne? It's Jojo. Can I come in?"

Leanne reacted to the hopeful sound in Jojo's voice by kicking the wall with her high heel.

Jojo poked her head in. She smiled, then glanced around at the mess. "What happened?"

"I moved in," Leanne said sarcastically.

Jojo stepped inside, something she had not done since Leanne had moved in. She was still wearing her cheerleading uniform under a red parka. Everything about her looked dreamy.

"Where are my clothes?" Leanne demanded.

"It's okay." Jojo slowly sat on the bed, as if she were moving through cotton. "My mom sent your things to the cleaners. Everything will be back tomorrow. You can borrow whatever you want of mine."

Leanne almost shot through the roof. Who knew if her clothes would survive a trip to the cleaners? She normally washed them out in her little sink and hung them in the window. "That's perfect."

"What do you mean?"

Leanne kicked one of Jojo's sister's shoes across the floor. "Now you want me to dress like you. Maybe you'd like me to go around school with 'Created by Jojo,' painted on my back."

Jojo's dreamy ease disappeared. "I don't know what you're talking about."

"I bet you know exactly what I'm talking about."

Jojo tried to smile.

"How was the swim meet?" Leanne hinted in a nasty voice.

"Actually, it was wonderful," Jojo replied. "You should have come."

"Right." Leanne pulled back for a moment. She wanted to tell Jojo exactly what she thought, but she didn't want to admit that she *had* attempted to go to the stupid meet. She'd walked down to the public pool, ready to face all the spirit heads and the dumb jocks in her moth-eaten fur. She'd showed up for Chip, and only for him. But before she'd even gone in, she'd overheard two girls gossiping.

"I'm telling you, it's about Jojo Hernandez," the first had said.

"How do you know that?" her friend had answered.

"Because I asked Brandy Kurtz which cheerleader it was. I went through the squad and when Jojo's name came up, Brandy went completely blank."

"That cinches it. But who's the homeless girl?"

"Well, then I talked to Lisa Avery and she said something about Leanne Heard, so it has to be her."

"Who?"

"You know, that weirdo girl who sang in the talent show."

"That's pretty amazing."

"What is?"

"That Jojo would take in a girl like that."

"Why is it amazing? Jojo is really generous. I used to think Jojo was kind of a lightweight. But not now. That took real guts, to take in somebody like Leanne."

"Jojo is special."

"Jojo is great."

Leanne glared right at great, special Jojo. "You think you have everything all figured out, don't you?"

"Me?"

"You've always had everything you ever wanted. I bet that since you were born there hasn't been one thing that you couldn't have."

"What makes you think that?" Jojo asked.

Leanne stomped through the mess she'd left and headed for her fur jacket, which she'd left near the door. "And now what you want is me as some kind of badge of generosity. I'm your charity of the month."

"How can you say that?"

Leanne finally reached the copy of *Bay News* that she'd stuffed into her pocket at the meet. She took the paper out and pitched it at Jojo. "You said it, not me. And if that wasn't enough, you had it published in the newspaper. Now you take this and stuff it."

The crumbled-up newspaper fell at Jojo's feet. She stared down, then picked it up and read it. "I didn't know he was going to make it so clearly about you and me. I didn't think anyone would know who he was writing about."

"Oh, come on," Leanne scoffed. "Just like you didn't know anything about getting rid of my clothes and trying to make me into some kind of trophy." She pushed past Jojo and grabbed her jacket.

"What are you doing?" Jojo managed.

"I'm going down to the amusement park, and don't tell me I shouldn't or I can't because you have no right to tell me anything," Leanne exploded. "You know nothing about me. You don't understand anything about the real world, and you never will!"

Leanne didn't stick around for Jojo's reply. She ran out, twelve blocks straight down to the promenade. Anything to get away from that

house, that bedroom, *that life*. It was all so surreal. Going from a sleazy rented room to upscale
suburban living and then back down to the arcade and the amusement park again.

First, she walked into the beachfront arcade,
one big room that screamed with the sound of
pinball machines, video games, and tiny bowling
alleys. Lights blinked. Clumps of kids hung out.
A vender sold stale popcorn, corn dogs on a
stick, and orangeade that always spilled and
made the floor sticky.

Leanne tried to adjust her eyes. The arcade
was a safe haven, but also a nightmare of lights
and noise and roaming kids who had nowhere
else to go. Leanne knew the place as if it were
her living room. She was practically a pinball
pro, and the people who worked there knew and
respected her. Nonetheless, she was too upset to
stick around. As soon as she walked in, she knew
she had to stay outside in the open air. That night
she needed the sweeping space of the amusement
park, the shrieks and rumbles of the big rides,
and the clean smell of the ocean.

After shouldering her way back out of the
arcade, Leanne jogged along the prom, past shell
and souvenir shops, until the lights of the roller
coaster loomed over her. Weaving through more

packs of kids, she slipped into the park's main entrance. Admission to the park was free, although the rides and games cost plenty. Because of that, Leanne didn't usually ride. She didn't play or eat. She just wandered in that otherworldly, magical place.

Once she was well inside the park, Leanne slowed down. She strolled by vendors and barkers, shooting galleries, Ferris wheels, the merry-go-round, Space Adventure Ride, Tunnel of Love, and the Wild Ride. She passed the booth that made up mock newspapers, where people could have their name made into a headline as having a two-headed baby or being Princess Di's long-lost sister. If Leanne had had any money, she might have had one printed up.

Leanne's Side of the Story: Drop Dead, Jojo.

"As if anyone cared," she muttered.

She found a vacant spot against the wire fence, looked back at the roller coaster, and thought about her side of things. Her life felt like that Big Thrill roller coaster. Every once in a while good things happened — like performing at the talent show and getting together with Chip. But she had to work so hard for those few victories. Chug, chug, chug, up the steep, difficult slope. She'd rest for a single second at the top, before the ride back down, which was so screamingly fast and easy. Then she would be down at the bottom again, lost and alone, while everyone else laughed and enjoyed the big thrill.

"Leanne! Is that you? LEANNE!"

Leanne looked around and spotted Ron McGyver, her friend who worked at the park. McGyver was waving, taking a break in front of the Laser Launch Spaceship in faded overalls and his old Giants cap. He met her in front of the Terminator Teacup Ride, which had been shut down and roped off.

"What's going on?" she asked.

"Hey." He smiled. "How are you? I haven't talked to you for a while."

"I haven't been around as much lately," Leanne answered. McGyver hung out at the Pelican Coffee Shop on the pier, and lots of street kids confided in him. Leanne knew that he'd helped a few kids get jobs or find a way back home. She stood next to McGyver for a few minutes, watching people stroll by with their pennants and cotton candy.

"I'm glad to see you," McGyver said. "I wanted to ask you something. Are you still working at the Tucker Resort?" McGyver asked.

Leanne didn't want to think about washing

dishes at Brent's family's resort. Brent had gotten her fired — for no real reason, except that she wouldn't let him treat her like dirt. She wondered what her next awful job would be, so that she could find another sleazy room to call her own.

"I'm not working anymore," she said.

McGyver frowned. "But you go to school with that Tucker kid, don't you?"

"Unfortunately. Why?"

He took a handkerchief out of his pocket and wiped his face. "No reason. Just that the Tucker kid — what's his first name? Brad?"

"Brent."

"Yeah. Well, he's been hanging around here, asking about the park."

Brent? The richest boy in Crescent Bay, hanging around the amusement park? "He has?"

"Yeah." McGyver rubbed his stubbly chin. "He wanted to know about the rides, about exactly when we were closing the park up, and what was going on. He was asking how we were going to shut the place up, how long the place would be closed down, weird stuff like that. I just thought it was kind of bizarre. Not too many kids come up to talk to me, then drive away later in their new BMWs."

Leanne couldn't quite follow what McGyver was saying. They were going to close the park! "What?" she gasped. "The park is closing?"

McGyver glanced back at the darkened Teacup ride. "Sure," he nodded. "Haven't you seen the notices?"

Leanne almost burst into tears. She didn't read notices when she came to the park. She just walked and daydreamed about being someone she'd never be.

"How can they close the park?" she cried. If she didn't have the park, what would she have in Crescent Bay? Where would she go? Especially now that she was stuck at Jojo's.

"It'll just be for a few weeks," McGyver assured her. "If we don't fix these rides up pretty soon, the place will get shut down for good. If you ask me, they should have fixed these rides before now."

Leanne was panicked. She could barely catch her breath. "When will you close?"

"Right away."

"But . . . but . . . what about the arcade?"

"The arcade will stay open." McGyver patted her shoulder. "Don't worry, kid. The park will open up again soon. This won't be permanent."

Leanne tried to tell herself that the arcade

would be enough. It had to be. But the news about the park had hit her like a punch in the stomach.

Finally McGyver gave her another pat. "You okay? I've got to get back to work. But I'll tell you when we open up again. If you need to talk before then, you know where to find me."

Leanne stood as still as a block of wood while Ron went back to work. She didn't want to think about Brent, or Jojo or that dumb newspaper anymore. The news that the park would temporarily be closed had thrown her into a tailspin.

Where was she supposed to go? She'd been forced to leave her mother's house, then she'd been fired from her job. Now the only home she had left was being shut down for repairs.

TEN

"Shhhhh! Do you want to get us thrown out of here?"

"Oh, Brandy, stop worrying so much."

"Lisa, Mrs. Daniels said she'd send us to the office if she caught us talking in here again. My parents will kill me if they get a phone call from Vice Principal Hud."

"Hud, shmud." Lisa giggled. "Mrs. Daniels was just having a cow that day. She usually doesn't even come out from behind her reference desk."

"Are you sure?"

Lisa slid down the end wall between the library stacks and waved her hand in disdain. "Brandy, sometimes I think you are the biggest baby."

Brandy winced. She hated hearing that, because she suspected that it might be true. Sophisticated Lisa never worried about dumb things like getting caught talking in the library. Lisa's tough, sexy shell always made her seem impervious to school rules and regulations. She could manipulate her way out of anything. Brandy always felt that everything she'd gained was tenuous. One wrong move and her entire power base at Crescent Bay High could be taken away.

Both girls looked at the lines of books on either side of them. Neither one of them liked to read. Lisa said all books were boring. The one good thing about the library was that they could go there during fourth-period study hall to gossip and hide out. The noise drove the librarians crazy, but there weren't enough of them to do anything about it.

"So, are your parents going to that open house deal tomorrow?" Lisa asked as she looked at her nails.

"My mom is. She really wants to see the squad do our dance routine."

"She would," Lisa scoffed. "I told my mom about it, and she told me she wanted to go about as badly as she wanted to tattoo her eyeballs."

Both girls snickered, and then snickered harder when they realized that if they didn't quit laughing they'd be caught. Finally they were pop-eyed and red-faced. Just when they were about to explode, they saw a curious face peering down from the other end of the stacks.

"Isn't that Simon Wheeldon Dealdon?" Brandy whined.

"WHO HE?" Lisa hooted, and they both started cracking up again.

"He's a junior," Brandy reminded her. "We saw him before the swim meet." When Lisa didn't react, she added, "He's no one."

Even so, Simon's red hair and freckles were unmistakable. His string tie flopped across his pearl-buttoned plaid shirt, and his baggy new jeans were dark as an eggplant.

"Hi," he said.

Both girls stopped snickering. Simon was not exactly one of their close friends, but he did have a reputation for being smart. His clothes were weird, but he knew tons of people. He was semi-nerdy, but he was also a person you could never quite peg.

Whatever he was, he looked like a boy with something on his mind. Brandy and Lisa waited to hear what it was.

Simon crouched down at their feet. "How's it going?" he whispered.

Lisa shrugged and began digging around in her bag. "It's going, Simon."

He cleared his throat. "Okay. Well . . . I hope I didn't interrupt anything."

"Who, us?" Lisa batted her lashes. "Heavens, no."

"I just wanted to ask you a couple of things," Simon said.

"We figured you didn't come by to check out a dirty library book," Lisa responded. She'd found a lipstick tube and began to dial up the color.

Simon blushed. "Remember just before the swim meet. You guys were talking about—"

"What!" Lisa hissed. "Were you listening to us?" She pointed the lipstick at him. "You know, turkey face, the last person who eavesdropped on one of my personal conversations lived to truly regret it."

Simon didn't seem too scared. "Yeah. I'm sure that's true. But you said at the swim meet that you saw Brent Tucker pull the fire alarm at that talent show a few weeks ago."

Brandy slapped her hand to her mouth, while Lisa shrugged. How could they have let anyone overhear that juicy piece of gossip? Brent would never have wanted anyone to know that! It was all Lisa's fault. Lisa could be so reckless.

"Don't you dare repeat that!" Brandy demanded.

"Brandy, shut up," Lisa snapped. "Why do you care, Simon?"

Simon crossed his freckled arms. "The reason I'm asking is because someone else got blamed for it. I don't call that fair."

"Who said life is fair?" Lisa fired back.

"Well, it's certainly fair for Brent Tucker," Simon said. "I'd say life is more than fair for him."

Lisa started to laugh. She kept laughing even after Brandy shushed her. She didn't stop until Mrs. Daniels rapped her pencil against the edge of her desktop.

"I'll agree with you on that one, Simon," Lisa said. "Tucker is spoiled scum as far as I'm concerned."

"Lisa!" Brandy objected.

Lisa gave her one of those don't-be-so-naive stares.

Simon began burrowing through his zippered case, in a way that reminded Brandy of her insurance executive father. Simon produced a piece of computer paper, then carefully trimmed off the dotted edges.

He pronounced in a very official-sounding voice, "I think you'll agree that Brent shouldn't get away with pulling the fire alarm and blaming it on someone else. I just want to get the facts straight," Simon went on. "It's called the truth."

Simon said it in such a straightforward tone that neither girl could answer right away.

Finally Lisa took a deep breath. "Okay, say we did see Brent do it. What's it to you?"

"LISA!" Brandy objected again.

Simon turned the piece of computer paper around, so that the girls could read it over. Brandy skimmed it quickly. She was appalled to read an official statement of Brent's guilt awaiting her and Lisa's signatures.

"This is sick!" Brandy whispered furiously. "You want us to rat on our friend! You are completely sick."

"Who said Brent was our friend?" Lisa grabbed the paper and looked it over, too.

Simon listened in silence, then unhooked a pen from his plastic pocket protector. He clicked it and handed it to Lisa.

"Lisa, don't you dare," Brandy begged.

Lisa ignored her. "Okay, Simon, what if we did see Brent do it. I'm not saying we really did, but for the moment, let's play pretend. Let's pretend that Brandy and I saw the whole thing."

"Okay," Simon nodded.

Lisa licked her lips. "Let's pretend Brandy and I ran to the back of the auditorium after our dance number at the talent show. Let's pretend that we wanted to watch that dimbo Leanne sing her song, and just happened to run by when Brent Tucker did the nasty deed."

Brandy couldn't believe what Lisa was doing. She was giving away everything.

"Supposing that all that is true—and I'm not saying it is—why should we sign this?" Lisa asked. "What do we get out of it?"

"You just said that Brent Tucker wasn't your friend," Simon said. "Here's your chance to make Brent suffer for what he did."

"How do I know that he'll really suffer?" Lisa asked. "How do I know this isn't just for you, Simon? Maybe you have some weird, private fetish where you like to collect documents on other kids."

Simon loosened his string tie and moved his neck around in his collar. "Because I'm going to give this to someone who will publish a story in the newspaper," he admitted. "Then everyone will know the truth. Brent Tucker will *have* to pay."

Lisa looked at Brandy. Brandy shook her head so hard that her frosted hair fell over her eyes.

Simon scooted closer, like a man about to open a treasure box who wanted nothing to get in the way. "Will you sign?" he insisted.

"NO!" Brandy exploded in a muffled scream.

"Not yet," Lisa said, finally acknowledging Brandy's fury. She took Simon's pen and tapped it against her lips. "Look, Simon. Now that I think about this, some other people are going to benefit from exposing Brent in the paper. Not just me. Didn't that sixties throwback, Chip Kohler, take the fall for Brent's prank?"

Simon shrugged.

Lisa twirled the pen around in her hand. "Well, I don't like hippie types. If you want me to help out Chip, you'll have to offer me something more than just Brent."

Brandy prayed that Lisa might be regaining her senses and giving up this whole thing.

Simon rubbed his freckled chin. "What else do you want?" he asked. "I don't see any reason why we shouldn't be able to make a deal."

"Good. Because I don't want anything else for myself," Lisa said. "I'm not selfish. I'd like something for my friend Brandy."

Brandy froze as she felt Lisa's arm slip around her. "For me?"

Simon grinned at Brandy. "No problem. What do you need?"

Lisa didn't give Brandy a chance to answer. "Since Chip is such a good friend of Jojo Hernandez's, how about if we ask Jojo to repay our favor. Jojo will owe one to Brandy."

"Jojo would owe *me* a favor?" Brandy choked.

"Exactly."

"I don't know," Simon worried. "Brandy, what would you want from Jojo?"

"Oh, nothing bad," Lisa assured him. "Brandy and Jojo are the best of friends. They're on the squad together. Brandy just needs a little weight for the next time they vote on new uniforms or a new dance move and there's a tie. That's all."

"That's really all?"

"Of course," Lisa said.

Simon thought for a moment. "Okay. That's a fair trade. If you sign this, then Jojo owes Brandy a favor. That's cool."

"Is it ever," Lisa confirmed.

There was a moment of silence, while Lisa scratched her name on Simon's document. Then she handed the pen to Brandy, who hesitated, but finally did the same.

"I don't know about this," Brandy said as soon as Simon had grabbed up the signed paper and rushed off.

Lisa turned to Brandy and pointed a finger. "Grow up, Brandy. You told me that Jojo has been driving you crazy. Well, here's your chance to get back at her. I just did *you* a favor. A big favor. Now, it's up to you to put your favor to good use."

"Scut time."

Chip heaved up the trash can and then dumped it over the edge of the school dumpster. The contents of the can fell in a satisfying rush of paper and junk, but Chip took no pleasure in a job well done.

"Slave work," he sighed.

It was the beginning of lunch period, and Chip was stuck. The open house was coming up and "Hud the Dud" had rounded him up and told him that he had to help get things ready. Chip was still paying for the fight after the school fire alarm prank, or at least what Hud thought had been a prank.

Chip hoisted the trash can back over his shoulder and headed back inside the school. He wished he could feel better about the work he was doing. He wished this was on a strictly volunteer basis. But even if it was, he wasn't sure it would matter. He would still have been too bummed out to take much pleasure in anything.

Leanne!

Why did Chip have to fall for such a difficult girl? Leanne hadn't just skipped the swim meet, she hadn't answered his phone calls, or even met him between classes. Jojo hadn't seen much of her, either. In fact, Jojo's father was starting to call Leanne the "stealth fighter." That was because Leanne was almost impossible to sight and when you did sight her you knew you were in hostile territory.

Chip didn't think that was too funny. But he got the point. Leanne was weird. She was mysterious and moody. He could never tell why she was so testy, or what had happened.

Should he put up with it?

Chip wondered. Should he try to talk to her? Should he issue an ultimatum, say, You'd better get your act together. No. Threats never worked on Leanne. When she was threatened she just put her back up because she knew that however bad it got she had already survived worse. And besides, Chip wasn't the macho type who'd demand a lot from her. He was the type to sit and wait and get walked on.

Chip lugged the trash can into the back of the school utility room. Mr. Moxler, the school engineer, had told him to go down to the gymnasium and start to set up chairs after that. So he headed down quiet, deserted hallways, looking at the smudged footprint marks on the waxed floor.

Chip was still staring at the smudges when he padded by the activity bulletin board near the guidance office. The only reason he stopped was that he saw Brent Tucker quickly take a note out of the pocket of his sports jacket and tape it over the section labeled Friends in Need.

Chip glared. The pit of his stomach went numb. His hands tingled. His legs buzzed with energy, and he felt a bead of sweat pop out on his forehead. What had they called this response in science class? *Flight or fight.*

Chip was ready to fight again! It was against his whole nature to admit it, but just seeing Brent had produced a violent reaction. Fortunately

Brent hadn't noticed Chip, although in some ways Chip would have liked him to. He would have liked to confront Brent again and ask him just what Brent had against him and Leanne.

But Brent was already gone. All he'd left behind was his note. Chip moved closer, as if he were being pulled by a magnetic attraction. He wasn't nosy by nature, but he'd learned to be interested in anything to do with Brent. Maybe that was related to another science class notion. *Survival of the fittest.*

Chip did a double take when he saw the note, because it was addressed to Miranda. He began to walk away, but that note seemed to be screaming at him from the other end of the hall. Written by the scum who hurt Leanne! it seemed to call out. Written to cause trouble for somebody else.

Halfway down the hall, Chip stopped. He'd never looked at someone else's note before. He'd never even read a piece of mail that hadn't been addressed to him. But this wasn't just any note. This was a note from the person who tried to ruin Leanne and then had almost gotten him kicked out of school.

Stiff as a robot, Chip turned around. Pushing down a horrible feeling, Chip reached for the note and read it.

Don't let me down. Remember: To-morrow night. In front of the fortune-teller place where Ocean Avenue meets the prom. I need to show you how life is one wild ride!

That was it. Chip stared at the message. The note had nothing to do with him. Nothing to do with Leanne.

But there was something about it that was threatening, nonetheless. Chip folded it back up and slipped it into the envelope again. Brent made Chip sick. He also made him very, very scared.

ELEVEN

"We'd better rehearse our routine," Gabe told Kat when he realized that lunch was almost over. "This open house thing is tomorrow."

Kat shrugged.

"Or maybe we should just mope." Gabe put on his Lounge Lizard voice. "And now, the Totally Hot comedy team brings all you teachers and parents The Mope." He put his fist under his chin and stuck out his lower lip.

Kat slapped his arm. "Gabe."

"Kaaaat."

She rolled her eyes.

Gabe wasn't sure what to do next. It was too nice a day to be cooped up in the cafeteria, so they were rehearsing in the middle of the soccer field. But Gabe wasn't really worried about their KHOT routine. They could always improvise.

It was their stupid date that needed careful planning. But before he could do that, he had to know whether they were on or off. If he didn't find out soon, he was going to lose his mind.

He'd done everything he could think of to get Kat's attention, but since her swim meet she'd been more distant than ever. Now she knelt on the field, pulling out blades of grass and putting them in little piles.

"Would you mind telling me what's on your mind?" he questioned.

She pulled out more grass.

"That was informative." Gabe glanced up at the sea gulls sailing overhead. "Let's go for Door Number Two. Would you mind telling me if we have a date tomorrow night?"

"What?"

He faced her again and shielded his eyes from the sun. "I asked you on a date, Kat. Remember? I know it was a shocking suggestion, but dating is a custom among other humans at this school."

"*Date*." Kat cringed. "I hate that word. It sounds like Date for trial. Date for sentencing. Date for execution."

"That's cheery."

She tossed the blades of grass into the air, and

they came down on her head. "Date. Yech. It's almost as bad as all those posters and things you did for my swim meet."

At least Kat was finally mentioning what he'd done at her meet. Until now, she'd been acting as if he'd stood on the top bleacher calling her dirty names. "Gee, thanks."

"Gee, you're welcome."

"You know, Kat. You could actually break down and really say thank you. That wasn't exactly my normal, everyday, rah-rah cheering for the swim team."

"Yeah, well, that wasn't my everyday rah-rah race." She started to get up, but he grabbed her hand. "Sorry, but I'm still in a bad mood about it."

"Master of the obvious."

Kat didn't laugh and wrenched her hand away. Gabe stared at her. "So what's your answer?"

"What answer?"

"What answer!" He pretended to pound his head against the ground. "The answer to the meaning of life. The answers to our Spanish quiz. What answer do you think, Kat? When someone asks someone else on a date they usually get a yes or no!"

She faced him. Her eyes looked watery and

totally confused. "Okay. Yes or no."

"Great."

"No . . . yes . . . no . . . yes," she blathered, shaking her head and making her necklace swing. "I don't know."

"Terrific," Gabe swore. "Is there anything else you want to tell me before we meet tomorrow? I'd at least like to know how I'm supposed to dress."

"Really," she grumbled. "Which black T-shirt and pair of black jeans."

"I've told you before, you want GQ, go out with Brent Tucker again."

She leaped to her feet and thrust her fist down at him. "That's not fair!"

"I'll show you fair," he dared.

"What?"

Gabe was going for the last resort. Kat had kissed him a while ago at a dance. She'd thrown herself at him in a huge liplock, only to prove something to Brent, then flounced away as if the kiss had been some under-the-mistletoe prank. Meanwhile, he'd been left with his head spinning and his heart booming away inside his chest. Talk about unfair!

Now it was time to return the favor. "Come here," he said, standing up.

"Why?"

"I want to show you something."

"What?"

"Don't be so suspicious."

She inched closer, glaring at him with folded arms.

Gabe glared back. "Look up."

"I know," Kat grumbled. "Look up, look down, look at my thumb, gee, you're dumb. Believe it or not Gabe, I was six years old, too. Only I've actually matured since — "

That was when Gabe did it — so fast that she couldn't have expected it. He put one hand on her shoulder, the other anchored around her back. First a fast kiss. Then, when her arms unfolded and her knees started to buckle he couldn't resist a much softer kiss, short and gentle.

Down fell Kat's book bag. Then her notebook and her thermos. Gabe recognized a single moment of being perfectly in synch until she put her palm flat against his chest and pushed him away.

"GABE!" she threatened, after she'd caught her breath. She fell to her knees and reached for her notebook.

He felt faint, too. And incredibly happy. "What?"

"I don't know," she cried as she gathered her things and began to run away. "I told you, I JUST DON'T KNOW!"

Something was finally happening to Jojo, but it wasn't what she'd yearned for. Since the previous night, she'd barely slept. Her head hurt. Her concentration wobbled.

Even her afternoon English class, which she usually liked, felt like torture. It wasn't that the teacher was boring, or that the subject — symbolism and the novel — was a drag. Jojo could have even stood sitting across from Brandy Kurtz, who kept giving her wicked little smiles, as if she'd rigged up a time bomb under Jojo's chair.

No, the part Jojo couldn't handle was Leanne. Leanne sat next to her, a well of brooding hostility. Since their fight over the newspaper article, Leanne had been acting like the human black hole — one that wanted to pull Jojo into negative space.

Jojo tried to listen to the lecture. Even though so many other things were zapping around her brain, she forced herself to watch the teacher's lips. She tried to memorize every word that had been printed on the board. But all she could think about was the wall of anger that had been put up by Leanne.

"Read the next three chapters for tomorrow," their teacher ordered as the bell went off. "And look at questions ten through twelve in your workbook!"

Jojo scooped up her books and made it out of the classroom only to find Brandy waiting just outside the door. Brandy was leaning back against a locker with her hands on her hips.

"Jojo, I have to talk to you," Brandy stated in a clipped voice.

"What about?" Since Jojo had stopped being a smile queen, Brandy had been pretty nasty to her. Maybe Brandy wanted to apologize . . . or maybe she just wanted to teach Jojo a new cheer.

Brandy looked up and down the crowded hall. "It's private."

Where were they supposed to go? The hall was as crowded as a Friday night dance. "Right now isn't a good time, Brandy. I have a test next period."

"Then how about after school today?" Brandy insisted.

Jojo knew exactly where she was going right after school, and Brandy was not part of that equation. "I can't. Sorry. How about tomorrow?"

Brandy huffed. "I can't tomorrow. I'll be running around all day getting ready for open house. We're doing a dance routine for the parents, remember?"

Jojo remembered . . . vaguely. "Look, Brandy, I have to go. Can't this wait?"

Brandy acted as if Jojo had asked her to postpone her next appointment to get her hair frosted. "No, it can't wait. I'll just have to find you again as soon as I can. I won't forget."

Goody for you, Jojo almost snarled as Brandy hurried off to flag down Lisa Avery, then followed Lisa into the girls' room.

Jojo headed straight to her last-period class. She somehow made it through her algebra test and handed it in early. But Mr. Amato still made her wait until the final bell. Then she trudged back up the stairs and headed for the journalism room.

"I don't want to do this," she sighed, holding back a huge lump of pain. "But I have to."

Jojo stopped on the middle of the stairway and let other kids pass. She was beginning to feel as if she'd been picked up, tossed around, then dumped into a ditch. As soon as she'd hugged Jackson that first day in the journalism office, she'd known she was in dangerous territory. If she wanted an experience, she'd certainly found one. Her feelings had leaped out, even though she'd known she should have held them back. Then Jackson had promised that he and Miranda were through. Miranda had confirmed the info. So the coast was clear, and from everything that Jojo got from Jackson at the swim meet, she could only assume that he was starting to feel the same way.

When Jackson had embraced her at that meet, Jojo had thought, Yes! Finally, I know what Kat and Miranda are talking about. And now I understand why they were so reluctant to share this with too many people! The feeling was so powerful, so scary that Jojo could see how it could make anyone do crazy, even dangerous things.

She waited for the traffic to clear, then climbed the rest of the stairs. She went right to the journalism room. Jackson was anything but alone this time. He was in the midst of his admiring staff, wearing a collarless shirt and army surplus pants. His whole staff must have torn over there after their last class, hoping to get the first word with him.

Jojo could make out a few of their questions as she entered.

"Jackson, would you read this and tell me what you think?"

"Jackson, which of these photos do you think is the best?"

"Do you think this cartoon makes sense, Jackson?"

"Jackson," Jojo said softly, not expecting to be heard.

But someone did hear her. And that staffer tapped the person next to her, who whispered to Sarah, the photographer. Suddenly they were all stepping aside as if Jojo were some kind of goddess.

She's the one . . .

That article of Jackson's . . .

I really admire her . . .

Jojo rushed over to Jackson.

"What's up?" he asked with a friendly smile.

Other newspaper staffers watched them, as if Jojo had come to deliver some deep, important message. She pulled Jackson toward the door. They walked far enough down the hall until the staff's rumble of noise turned into a low, even hum.

"Did you find out something?" Jackson wanted to know.

Jojo forced herself not to wear her please-like-me smile. "You could say that."

"What's the matter?" he prodded. "Did something happen with the Brent story?"

"No." She turned away from him. "And nothing's going to happen."

"What do you mean?" Jackson objected. "We have to keep working on it. We have to nail Tucker!"

"I don't have to do anything," Jojo argued. "I don't want to work on the story anymore."

Jackson ran his hand through his spiky hair. "Wait a minute. Why not? What's going on?"

"That's just what I want to know," she replied. "Why didn't you tell me you were making that story about me and Leanne so obvious? Everyone knows that it was about us."

Jackson looked confused. "I did tell you. I distinctly asked you if it was all right."

"I didn't know exactly what you were going to print!"

"Jojo, I didn't use your name."

"It doesn't matter!" Jojo argued. "People know. I don't know how they know, but they do. And I'm not the one who matters here. What about Leanne?"

Jackson went pale. He moved away from her,

then slumped down onto the hall floor with his face in his hands. "Oh, my God," he breathed. "I didn't think."

"You didn't think," Jojo repeated. "You just pushed ahead and didn't consider that you were pushing Leanne along with you."

"I'm sorry." He suddenly looked up, as if he'd realized something else entirely. He thought for a moment with wide eyes. "I'm so sorry," he whispered.

Jojo was sorry, too. She was sorry that she'd sacrificed Leanne just to please Jackson, and that her feelings for him were getting so out of control. Now she wasn't sure what to do. Jackson was on one side of her, and Leanne was on the other. She felt as if she were about to be crushed in the middle.

Suddenly Jackson looked up when they both heard someone running up the stairs. A moment later, Simon Wheeldon appeared. He was so out of breath that he looked as if he were going to keel over and tumble back down.

"You're here. I found you," Simon Wheeldon gasped. "I thought I'd miss you for sure."

"Simon!" Jojo said. "What is it?" She'd barely given Simon a second glance since they'd sold ads together weeks before.

Jackson slowly stood up.

Simon kept his eyes on Jojo. "I found out right before lunch, but I couldn't find you right away and then we had these presentations in my Practical Business Skills class last period, and we went overtime, and I thought I'd never get out of there and find you." He flopped over to catch his breath.

"Why would you want to find me?" Jojo asked.

"Read this," Simon said, handing her an official-looking sheet of paper.

Jojo glanced back at Jackson before unfolding the page.

"It doesn't matter how I knew you needed this," Simon explained with embarrassment. "I just knew that you wanted a witness who saw Brent Tucker pull that fire alarm at the talent show. Well, I have two witnesses for you. Signed, sealed, and delivered. Here's their statement, and you can even print it if you want to." He handed over the paper with a proud, expectant smile.

When Jojo saw Brandy's and Lisa's names at the bottom of the page, her knees almost buckled. Her mood did a one-hundred-and-eighty-degree turn. Then her feelings flip-flopped once more when she sensed that Jackson had moved in close and was looking over her shoulder.

"This changes everything," she cried. "Look!" She wanted to scream so loudly that she would be heard in the next town, while at the same time she wanted to curl up against Jackson and not make a sound at all. She tipped her face up to his, eager to see his reaction to their incredible good fortune.

At the same time Jackson leaned over further, and suddenly he was looking right at her. He smiled. She held her breath. Everything stopped, as if she had gone into slow motion. Her eyes closed. Her breathing slowed. Her lips parted. She moved closer.

And then it happened. Her mouth brushed against Jackson's. It was barely a kiss, and much more than a kiss at the same time. It was a whisper, a breeze. Jojo couldn't believe she'd really done it. All she knew was that, with Simon Wheeldon looking on, her life had just been changed for good.

TWELVE

Miranda pushed open her kitchen door and looked out at the rumbly ocean. The sun was setting, and she could see the fog pouring in. The air was cooling down fast.

"Miranda, are you taking off already for the open house?" her father called to her.

"Uh, yes, Dad. I'm on my way."

"How come you're leaving so early?"

"No reason," she lied, staring out at the dusky promenade. A half mile down the beach and she'd meet Brent. Even if she were prepared to tell her father the truth, she couldn't have given him a straight answer. Because she didn't understand why she was going to meet Brent, and she didn't know what was going to happen when she did meet him.

Her dad neatened his tie, then looked at Miranda by way of the hallway mirror. "It's all right. I know how you always have to be at these school events way before anyone else." He smiled proudly. "That's my Miranda."

"Right." Miranda wondered if she would be "his Miranda" if her father knew where she was really headed. She was still spooked by the fact that Brent had asked to meet her in front of that old fortune-teller's shop. Her father associated funky beach places like that with major world calamities like flood, fire, and famine.

"Are you sure you don't want to wait for a ride?" her father asked. "Your mom and I can drop you fairly soon, on our way to the city council meeting, if you can just hold on a few minutes."

"Thanks, Dad. But I want to walk."

He checked his shave. "You know, your mom can't come to your open house. I'm dropping her off at the city planning meeting, but I'll swing by and hear your welcome speech."

"Thanks," Miranda sighed. Her mom was so busy lately with her real estate job; Miranda hadn't expected that night to be any different.

"But I can't stay long," her dad added. "Your mother wants me to join her back at the meeting as soon as you're done."

Miranda had already stepped outside. She felt

damp air against her face. "Okay," she called back. "See you later. I'm going. 'Bye."

She gave one last wave and then she was fleeing along the prom, aware of that same fierce pounding in her chest that she used to feel when she snuck out to meet Jackson. As she ran, she wondered why she was in such a panic. It wasn't that she was eager. It wasn't that she was afraid of being late for her meeting with Brent. Maybe it was just that she was afraid — period — and she was trying to outrun the feeling once and for all.

She trotted in a wavy line, dodging tourists and baby carriages, dogs and old people out for their evening walks. As she ran, the few wispy clouds turned into a solid bank of fog. By the time she reached downtown, she could no longer see the water.

She wandered a short way up Ocean Avenue, not quite remembering where the fortune-teller's shop was. When she passed the arcade she was hit with a wall of sound and blinking light, which faded as soon as she passed by again. She looked across the street, and sure enough, Brent was waiting for her, leaning back against the store window that was stenciled *Emilia's* —

Guidance for All. The wind coming off the ocean tossed his golden hair. When he saw her he lifted his thumb and one finger, then gestured as if he were shooting a gun.

Miranda crossed the street to meet him. When she got there Brent cocked his head and offered an innocent smile. He unrolled his turtleneck, pushing it way up to keep out the wind, which had turned surprisingly cold.

"Ready?" Brent asked.

"Ready for what?"

"Ready for anything." His smile widened. He reached for her hand.

"What do you mean?" She avoided his touch by pretending to shiver. She hugged herself.

"Don't worry," he soothed. "You're so jumpy."

"I am not," she lied. "I just thought you wanted to talk."

"I do."

She glanced into the fortune-teller's shop and saw drapes, strange, eerie pictures, and old, stuffed chairs. Then she looked back at the blinking, noisy arcade across the street.

"You want to go in there?" Brent asked, pointing to Emilia's, the fortune-teller's.

She shook her head.

"Okay." He gestured to the arcade. "How about over there?"

"No! I want to talk," she repeated. "I'm supposed to be your peer counselor. Isn't that what this meeting is all about?"

He faced her and ran his fingers lightly down her arms. "Is it?"

"Is what?" she asked, really starting to tremble.

"Is this just about me and my boring problems?" He pretended to pout.

"Of course it is!"

Brent pulled her against him. "Then why are you shaking?"

Why was she shaking? Why was she even there? Why hadn't she taken his note from the Friends in Need board and thrown it away? And why was she letting him hold her?

"I'll tell you why," Brent whispered in her ear before she could answer her own questions.

She stood very still, trembling, and feeling his heart thumping against hers.

"Because in some weird way, you have something to prove and someone to get back at," he said. "Just like I do. And you know that I can help you do it."

"What?" she asked, even as she felt herself melt into Brent and allow him to intertwine his fingers with hers.

"You're such a good girl," he went on in a mesmerizing voice. "I'll bet you've always been a good girl. I'll bet that everyone just assumes you'll be that way forever."

Miranda couldn't help thinking that her father had certainly felt that way . . . until she'd struck out on her own by running off with Jackson. But then Jackson felt that way, too, when she didn't have the guts to stick it out.

Brent pressed his cheek against hers. "Just once, wouldn't you like to do something so crazy, so wild, that you could prove them all wrong?"

Miranda didn't answer.

"Wouldn't you?" he insisted.

Miranda closed her eyes and tried to clear her mind. She tried to think. Finally she leaned into Brent and ran with him through the heavy fog.

The Crescent Bay High gymnasium was decorated with a "tree of learning," something like a huge Christmas tree, only with books instead of ornaments. There were graphs and posters, and a booth where Chip ran a short video for ten people at a time. Some parents were still arriving, while others milled around. At the same time, Jojo and the squad launched into the big finish of their dance routine.

"Let's thank the cheerleaders for that wonderful performance," projected Roslyn Griff, student body president.

Patches of applause.

"Before we get started with our formal program," Roslyn continued, "we have some more entertainment for you. Please welcome the Crescent Bay High Tintypes Jazz Band!"

Jojo jumped off the stage and bounded down the aisle to join Jackson. Since they'd found out about Simon's witnesses, Jojo had wiped thoughts of Leanne out of her head. Not that Leanne wasn't important, but Jojo's first priority was Jackson . . . and their article, of course. She'd stayed up all night writing a first draft of their story. Never before had she written with such energy, such purpose. The words had flowed out of her, and she wasn't even tired. She'd called her story "Pulling a Switch."

Jojo dropped into the chair next to Jackson's. He was holding her story in front of him. Unable to hold back, she asked, "How is it?"

Jackson rustled the paper.

Jojo panicked. The idea of Jackson not liking her story suddenly terrified her. "I didn't know if you wanted someone on your staff to write this, but I thought I'd at least give it a try," she chattered nervously. "After I got home last night, I thought about how mad I felt and what I should do about it. I wish I could do something to make it all up to Leanne, but she won't give me a chance. So I decided to write that article instead."

He read it over one more time.

"It's awful, isn't it," she panicked.

"Are you kidding?"

"What?"

He glanced up at her. "Jojo, this is good. Really good. I can't believe you've never written for a newspaper before."

That old fizzy feeling was back, multiplied by ten with the memory of how she'd kissed him. "I took creative writing and wrote ads for about a dozen school fund-raisers." She slid closer and leaned against his shoulder. "It is really okay?"

"Okay?" Jackson nudged her. "Okay! If one of my staffers came up with a first draft like this, I'd jump up and down with joy."

"Really?"

He nodded. "Absolutely."

Her eyes lingered on his. She wanted to stay in the moment forever, to freeze frame it and never leave. She still couldn't believe that her life had really been transformed. All she knew was that Jackson had helped transform it, and that she now understood everything that Kat and Miranda had ever talked about. No longer was something missing from her life. On the contrary. Now she felt so full that she was bursting at the seams.

She took back her article as Jackson picked up his open house program and stared into it. "Is Miranda here?" he asked. "This says that she's the welcome speaker."

Jojo quickly looked up from her typed pages. "I haven't seen her yet. Why?"

"No reason."

"She must be here somewhere, I guess." Jojo leaned toward the aisle, then peered down at Chip's video booth. "There's her father." Slowly she peeled off her spirit gloves and offered a wave to Mr. Jamison.

"That's her father?" Jackson repeated. He followed Jojo's gesture, spotting a tanned, slender man wearing a three-piece suit and tie. Jackson felt his stomach clamp down. "You know, the whole time I was with Miranda, I never really met her father," Jackson admitted. "There was this big thing between us, but he would never even shake my hand. Maybe now that things are finally over with Miranda, the time has come."

Jojo stared, then looked down. "Go ahead. If you really want to. I'll read this over again."

Jackson wove his way through the parents and teachers, hoping that he was heading for the right person after all. He'd only seen Mr. Jamison from a distance. In the past, the sight of Mr. Jamison leaving the house had been a green light for Jackson to run and meet Miranda.

When he found Mr. Jamison, he walked right up and stuck out his hand. "Excuse me," Jackson said, his pulse racing. "I'm Jackson Magruder. A friend of Miranda's."

Mr. Jamison didn't register anything. He ignored the invitation to shake hands.

Jackson cleared his throat. "At least I used to be a friend of Miranda's. A very good friend."

Mr. Jamison finally made the connection. He frowned and stepped back, taking in every inch of Jackson's old sweater, jeans, cartoon-covered tennies, and leather jacket. "What are you doing here?"

He'd asked it as if Jackson were some kind of dropout or druggie who would never attend anything as reputable as a parent/teacher open house. "I'm covering this for the school newspaper. I'm the paper's editor," Jackson said.

"You are? Miranda never told me that."

You mean, you didn't want to know, Jackson felt like saying. All you wanted to know was that I rode a skateboard, dressed weird, and wasn't a football team captain like Eric Geraci.

"Yeah . . . well," Jackson sighed.

Mr. Jamison peered around the gym, with his hands set on his hips. For a few moments neither he nor Jackson spoke.

Mr. Jamison finally broke the silence. "I wonder where Miranda is. I haven't seen her here yet. Have you?"

Jackson shook his head.

"She left home so early," Mr. Jamison explained. "She's probably just working overtime on something. I'm proud of how hard she works. I know I push her, but I think she likes it. Mostly, she pushes herself."

Jackson had to wonder if both he and her father hadn't encouraged Miranda to push herself even further. Not that a girl as driven as Miranda was all that susceptible. But she had to prove to herself that she could do any- and everything.

Mr. Jamison stuck his hands into his pockets

and shifted. "Miranda is very ambitious, and I think that's good. That's why I'm so particular about how she spends her time. And who she spends it with. I just care so much."

Jackson stared at him. "I care, too," he heard himself say. "A lot."

Mr. Jamison stared back and neither of them said another word. Jackson was stuck wondering why he'd suddenly made that declaration and exactly what it meant. But before he could figure it out, they were interrupted by Kat, who was dressed to do a KHOT routine in a top hat and drama department tux.

"Hi, Mr. Jamison," Kat said in a funny voice. She glanced briefly at Jackson.

"Hi, Kat," Mr. Jamison said. "Where's your radio partner?"

Kat pointed to Gabe, who was watching the video with Chip. She forced a smile. "Listen, Mr. Jamison, I wanted to let you know that there's been a change in the schedule."

"Oh?"

Kat bounced on her desert boots. "See, well, Miranda had to help with some . . . important stuff, so Gabe and I are going to give the welcome speech instead. I don't know when Miranda will give her speech. Whenever she's done with her important stuff . . . I guess."

Mr. Jamison looked around the gym, then checked his watch. He refused to look back at Jackson. "All right. I can't really hang around, so I guess I'd better get going. Tell Miranda I was here and that I'll see her later."

"I will."

"Good to meet you, Mr. Jamison," Jackson said, blocking Mr. Jamison's path and sticking out his hand.

Finally Mr. Jamison reached for Jackson's hand and pumped it in a firm, businesslike way. "Nice to meet you, Jackson."

After letting go of Mr. Jamison's hand, Jackson turned back to catch Jojo's eye. She gave him her usual warm, glowing smile.

Kat immediately gestured for Jojo to join them, then leaned in and whispered, "Miranda's not here at all, you guys!"

"She isn't?" Jackson sounded panicky.

Kat shook her head. "I don't know where she is. She'd never be late, especially when her father didn't know where she was. Gabe and I will cover for her speech, but I have the feeling that something might be wrong."

Jojo moved closer to Jackson. "What do you think?" she asked in a breathless voice.

Jojo slipped her hand into his, as he thought only of Miranda. He had already figured out that he and Miranda were still connected. He'd even begun to realize that he was still in love with her. And now he knew, deep in his heart, that something was terribly wrong.

THIRTEEN

"I guess I have to let you off the hook, Kohler," Vice Principal Hud barked to Chip, as the open house formally got off the ground. "Now get this video equipment put away and your probation is finished. But don't let me catch you trying anything else in my school again."

Your school, Chip thought. As if Hud personally owned the library books and the Bunsen burners.

Hud continued to loom over him. "And don't forget to rewind that videotape."

"Right," Chip mumbled.

"And make sure you leave that machine exactly as you found it."

"Yes, sir." Did Hud think Chip was going to steal the knobs off the TV? Maybe reset the VCR so it only taped episodes of morning cartoons?

Hud glared at Chip, then wandered back to patrol the back of the gymnasium, as if he were going to monitor the parents for talking.

Chip pulled the TV and VCR plugs out of the wall socket, then dropped everything back on the audiovisual cart. It took all of his self-control not to dump the machines on the gym floor. Meanwhile, Kat and Gabe launched into their routine, which had been moved up to replace the very bizarre no-show by Miranda.

As usual, Kat and Gabe were funny, but Chip wasn't in a joking mood. For once he wasn't only thinking about Leanne. No, this time he focused on himself as well. And he didn't need any science class to understand what was going on this time.

He was angry.

Even Mr. Mellow, Chip Kohler, could boil over if he were pushed hard enough. Chip was the first one to acknowledge that he'd broken a school rule when he'd punched Brent. Hey, he knew he had to pay the consequences. But Hud had been acting as if Chip had been caught selling drugs to sixth-graders. The VP seemed to have wiped out the fact that Chip was still a B-plus student, still the junior who'd organized the re-cycling campaign for the entire school, still a

polite and decent guy! Because of that one stupid
fight — which hadn't even been Chip's fault —
Hud thought he had the right to treat Chip like
dirt.

Chip coiled the TV and VCR cords and threw
them on the back of the cart. Waves of laughter
floated through the gym while Kat did her comedy number and Gabe played straight man. Kat
and Gabe were doing their war-of-the-sexes
thing, which all the parents thought was a laugh
riot. But it just made Chip think even more
about the war between Hud the Scud, himself,
and Leanne.

Chip realized that he was no longer acting so
politely, or even so decently. Between Leanne
and Hud, he couldn't hold it together anymore.
The more Hud had ragged him, the more sullen
and resentful he'd become. Eventually, he'd been
reduced to one-syllable grunts. Even if Leanne
herself had walked in right then, Chip might not
have spoken to her. The only way he would have
been able to relate would have been to hold her
or to kiss her. He was too angry for anything
besides primitive, physical contact.

Chip slumped down next to the audiovisual
cart. How many people treated Leanne the way

Hud had been treating him? How long had it taken for her to perfect her defensive style? Maybe Chip had even been making it worse by insisting that Leanne join his friends, as if he owned her social life, the way Hud thought he owned their school.

Chip sat with his chin on his fist and thought. He might have stewed through the whole open house if Jojo hadn't tiptoed up to him and tapped his shoulder. He tried ignoring her, then even backed away from her touch, hoping that she would go away.

"Chip, I need to talk to you," she whispered, not giving up.

He still wanted to grunt and mope, until he saw something in Jojo's eyes that he'd never seen before. He wasn't sure what it was, but it jolted him out of his horrible mood.

Jojo gestured for him to follow her out to the foyer. Chip trailed her, plodding past eager parents and tired teachers. He didn't really wonder what was going on until they stepped into the gym foyer. There, among the trophy cases and game schedules, was Jackson Magruder. Usually Chip thought of Jackson as savvy and cool, but Jackson looked about as cool as a first-time freeway driver. His leather jacket was stuffed under his arm, as if he needed to make a quick getaway. He looked terrified.

Chip took in Jojo again. That new something was still there, glistening in her bright eyes. Everyone had been gossiping about the new Jojo lately, as if she'd suddenly turned into Debbie DoGooder. Chip didn't believe in total personality change. He just saw his old, dear friend Jojo with something added. This was Jojo with more guts.

"Did you drive your van here tonight?" Jojo asked him in a frantic voice.

Chip nodded. "Sure. Why?"

Jackson started to answer, but Jojo interrupted. "Jackson is worried about Miranda not showing up for this." She glanced briefly at Jackson, then looked down at the Sea Lion emblem inlaid in the floor. "I'm worried, too. We have to do something. I don't know what, but can we at least borrow your van and drive around and look for her?"

Chip remembered the note he'd read on the Friends in Need board. The note didn't tell exactly where Miranda would be, but it sure did point to Brent Tucker and that fortune-teller's place by the beach. And that was enough to make him worry, too.

"I think I might know something," he said as he reached in his pocket for his keys. "My van is in the parking lot. You're right to be worried. Let's go."

Miranda hadn't climbed a fence since seventh grade, when Kat had convinced her to sneak into their middle school. That fence hadn't been nearly as high as the one that surrounded the amusement park. And it certainly hadn't been topped with a roll of barbed wire.

Brent let go of her hand and pointed to a three-foot break in the wire. He'd somehow scouted out the one place where it was possible to climb over. "Here's the place," he said. "Up and over. Let's take a private tour."

"I thought you just wanted to look at the park," Miranda panicked. She'd only gone to the amusement park with him because he'd wanted to show her how amazing it looked with everything shut down and turned off. She'd never thought that he would want to sneak in.

Brent grinned. "I changed my mind."

He climbed easily, jumping up and making

the fence shake so loudly that Miranda was sure they would get caught. He reached the very top, then leaped down in one movement. When he hit the ground, he rolled in a somersault and laughed.

Then he spun back to face her through the fence. "Your turn, good girl."

Miranda knew that this was her chance to back out. She'd already missed showing up for her welcome speech. Her father must have noticed her absence, so maybe she'd already proved to him — even to herself — that she couldn't always be perfect, successful Miranda.

Brent stuck his fingers through a metal link and tugged the hem of her sweater. He pushed his face against the fence. "Don't leave me alone in here."

She tried to pull away, but he clung to her. "Why?"

"I don't know what I'll do if you leave me." He held onto her sweater as if he wanted to rip it to shreds. "Don't forget, you're my peer counselor. You're responsible for me."

"Oh, come on."

"You come on," he wooed. "Climb the fence. Don't desert me. Don't chicken out. Don't fail me now."

Brent rattled the fence again. Miranda knew that she should turn around and run home, or try to get to school before the open house was over. But for some reason, she reached up and began to climb, too. It wasn't as easy as she remembered. The soles of her riding boots slipped. Her grasp was unsure. She caught her sweater on the chain link, then tore the sleeve when she unhooked herself and carefully climbed down.

Brent was there to catch her. As she lowered herself, his hands slid around her waist and soon she was standing nose to nose with him, while he laced two fingers through the belt loops of her jeans.

Miranda pushed him away and looked around. She hadn't been to the park since the previous summer, when Kat had met that out-of-town boy. Miranda remembered a seedy but lively place, crowded and dirty, full of sweet smells and wild noise. What she saw now was altogether different. The light came from the few scattered street lamps that cast long, fuzzy shadows. The game booths were all boarded up. Plastic tarps were roped around the vending stands. The rides were frozen in midcycle, topped by a fog that was settling in over the bay.

"There's no one here at all," she whispered, spooked by the unnatural quiet. The only sounds were the ocean crashing against the nearby pier and the squawk of the occasional sea gull.

"I know." Brent stretched his hands up into the fog. He began to stroll. "I snuck in last night to check it out. I thought there'd be security guards or something, but there's only one cop at the main entrance." He stopped to grin back at her. "IT'S JUST YOU AND ME," he yelled. Then he spun around a lamppost, finally running back, and grabbing her around the waist again.

She grasped his hands, trying to get him to talk to her for once. She held onto one last hope that she could counsel him.

"Why did you sneak in last night?" she asked. "Why would you even think of coming here when it's all closed down?"

He stood still for a moment and for once his face was dead serious. "What else is there to do around this town? Play pinball? Surf? Buy little shells at one of those tourist shops and make a wall hanging? I don't know why my parents ever had to open a resort here. I don't really know anyone here. This place makes me crazy." He turned away and kicked the ground.

This time he walked ahead of her, in a straight

line, as if he knew exactly where he was going
and wasn't going to stop until he got there.
When he was two rides away, Miranda started
to get scared again. Brent was ready to leave her
behind, if he had to. Was she really going to
climb that fence again and sneak back out alone?
What if that cop caught and arrested her? She
wasn't allowed to visit this place on a July afternoon, let alone at night when it was shut down
for repairs.

She pulled her sweater tightly around herself
and ran, catching up to Brent in front of the
roped-off attraction called the Wild Ride. He had
climbed over the rope border and was examining
the ride's controls.

Miranda held the rope down and climbed
over, too. She joined him, amazed at how big
the Wild Ride looked when she stood underneath
it. It was probably forty feet tall, like some giant
barbell. The ride was old, one that probably gave
a gut-wrenching thrill just by flinging people up
and down. The frame was a long, fat pipe,
painted with red, white, and blue stripes. On
either end was a capsule, decorated with stars
and big enough to hold two people.

Brent stared down at the control, which con-
sisted of buttons and two large throw switches,

painted red. He leaned against one switch, which started a rumbly motor. Then he walked over to the capsule that hung close to the ground and opened the half door.

"Care to take a spin with me?" he dared, gesturing to the capsule.

"Are you crazy?"

He smiled. "I thought you'd know the answer to that by now."

Miranda didn't move. The capsule was made of metal, covered with peeling paint. Inside was a single bench and two sets of seat belts.

Brent slowly walked back from the capsule and circled around her. Then he lifted her hair and kissed the lobe of her ear. "Let's go for a ride," he whispered.

"No!" she cried.

He held her shoulders and pushed his face against her neck. "I'll get in with you. If it was really dangerous, I wouldn't get in, would I?"

She didn't answer, but instead tried to shake free of his grip.

"I can't go alone, Miranda. What if this thing throws me way up high and I decide to jump out? I'll need you."

"You don't need me!"

"Then maybe you need me."

"What?"

"Why are you here?" he challenged. He turned her around so that they were face-to-face. His fingers dug into her arms. "You knew I didn't just want to talk to you. You knew that something was going to happen, and that's exactly what you wanted, good girl. That's why you're here."

His hands pressed even harder as he leaned in to kiss her. Miranda pushed away from him with all her strength, but he held on hard, weaving one hand through her hair so that she could barely turn her head. She wanted to run away. She wanted the whole night to go away. But she didn't know where to go . . . what to do. She was alone and stupid and caught.

"Let me go," she threatened.

He pressed against her and began kissing her neck. Even as she began to cry, he held on harder, gripping her back and pushing against her.

Finally she kicked his shin, then slammed her elbow into his gut. As he stumbled back, she rushed into the capsule. Brent laughed, then threw the second switch before jumping in with her, like some old-time western actor jumping on his horse. He gave a rodeo holler as the contraption took off. The door wasn't even all the way closed as they slowly rose into the air. Then the capsule began swinging them up and down, up and down. It spun around, then went up and down again.

Brent fell against Miranda, pushing into her with each jolt. The park spun beneath her. She was dizzy — sick to her stomach. But she could only think about finding and fastening her seat belt so that she wouldn't be thrown out.

"YAHOOO!" Brent leaned out the window, and yelled his head off. Miranda scrambled for the belt. It pinched her fingers as she fastened it. Just then Brent fell back on her lap, then onto the capsule floor. There was a jerk. Then a slight wobble side to side. The fog settled. The wind blew. The Wild Ride had stopped, dangling them forty feet over the blacktop.

"What happened?" Miranda gasped.

Brent howled. He leaned out the window, hooting to the ocean and the abandoned rides. "We're stuck," he laughed. "Broken down!"

Miranda curled into the corner and began to cry. She was such a fool. Why had she ever gotten in? Why had she ever been attracted to Brent? She was suddenly desperate to see Jackson's face and wondered what had she been trying to prove.

Ping, ping, ping . . .

Leanne was surrounded by pinball, foosball, and video games. She breathed in the smell of caramel corn and cigarettes. She was used to the harsh neon, the blinking lights, the TILT alerts and the people wandering in and out looking for the game that would distract them for a while and make the problems in life go away.

I wish I could distract myself forever, and make my life go away, period! she thought.

She'd been at the arcade since right after school, no easy feat considering that she'd only brought two dollars. She'd needed to stretch her quarters, because she needed time to think. She felt disconnected. Mismatched. Sure, Chip was great, but he wanted everything on his terms. Jojo probably meant well, too — in her weird way — but she just didn't get it and maybe she never would.

"Hey, Leanne."

Leanne looked up. It was Jimmy Raye Horton, one of the arcade regulars. He lived on the street some of the time. Other times he got jobs at the motels and lived there.

"Hi, Jimmy."

"What's doing?" He came up to her in his greasy hooded sweatshirt, dirty jeans, and open, unlaced high-top tennis shoes. He was unshaven and sleepy-looking, and he knew how to make one game of pinball last forever. Nonetheless, he was always looking for Leanne and asking advice.

"You know, I was just hanging out with McGyver over at the Pelican. He said he'd seen you," Jimmy said. "I haven't seen you around here much lately."

Leanne shrugged. "It's a long story."

Jimmy didn't demand an explanation. Instead he asked, "Want to go over and play a game on the Cyclone?"

"Sure." The Cyclone was the best pinball machine in the arcade. Leanne was considered something of an expert at it. She and Jimmy had played games late at night that sometimes had gone on for hours.

Leanne would have liked to lose herself in a good game of Cyclone. Fixing herself on a little steel ball propelling back and forth between whirling gates sounded just great. But just as Jimmy offered her her first turn, she looked up and out the arcade window.

Her reaction was so strong that Jimmy looked, too. Chip, Jojo, and Jackson Magruder were standing across the street in front of Emilia's. They talked, then paced, then talked again. From their body language, Leanne guessed that they were in some kind of panic. For a moment she stopped her game and remembered seeing another pair in front of the same window, earlier that evening: Brent and Miranda. Even she had sensed that something weird was going on between those two, and she had to wonder if that was why Chip, Jojo, and Jackson were there.

"Who are they?" Jimmy asked.

Leanne stared a little while longer. "It doesn't matter," she finally said. "They're certainly not down here to pay me a visit."

She went back to her game with Jimmy. Let them stand on Ocean Avenue forever, she decided. Chip could stand there all night, if he didn't have the decency to cross the street and enter her turf.

FOURTEEN

Kat and Gabe were in the boys' locker room. While the open house dragged on inside the gym, Gabe had charmed one of the coaches into letting them both use the locker room to change out of their KHOT costumes. Kat knew that the moment had come. Date or no date. No more indecision. Unfortunately her heart was still walking both sides of the fence.

She sat on a bench in the tights and leotard she'd worn under her tux. A sweatshirt was tied around her waist, and her costume was in a heap on the floor. Gabe, meanwhile, stood in front of his gym locker, pulling on a clean T-shirt.

"Gabe, would you mind telling me what the rush was to get out of the gym?" she asked, still hoping to avoid the real issue.

Gabe threw his sweaty T-shirt into his locker.

"Are you telling me you wanted to stick around for Mr. Melman's speech on education in the computer age?"

"No," she grumbled. "I just didn't want to be rushed around like I was a shopping cart or something."

He huffed and kicked the locker door. "Kat, if you think you're a shopping cart, that's your problem. I certainly have never thought of you as a shopping cart."

"I know." She groaned. "You know what I mean!"

"No, Kat. Actually I don't." He slammed his locker shut and faced her. "Do *you* know what you mean?"

Kat threw up her hands and began to pace. "Never mind. I'm just worried about Miranda."

"Jojo, Jackson, and Chip went to look for her. There's nothing for us to do," he reminded her.

"I know."

"Besides, I don't think that's what you're really bugged about."

"How do you know?" She hopped onto the thin bench that ran down Gabe's locker corridor and walked it like a balance beam.

"Kat," he stated, "I know more about you than you think."

She jumped off the bench and glared at him. "You do not."

"Do, too."

"Do not!"

He threw up his hands. "Well, now that we've finished another mature discussion, maybe you can finally tell me if we're going out tonight, or if I should just stop at the Burger Barn and head on home."

"I DON'T KNOW!"

"Great," he swore, sitting with his back to her. He dropped his head into his hands. "Just great. Thank you very much. I really hope we do this again."

Kat knew she was acting like a jerk. But she still couldn't deal with it. Heck, she should have given Gabe an answer days ago, but her head was still reeling from losing the race. And after Gabe had kissed her on the field, her head had spun so much that she'd almost left the planet.

Maybe other girls wanted to leave the planet, but not her. Not now, anyway. She'd spent enough time out there in the emotional stratosphere and for once she wanted some nice, calm time down on good, old Earth. She didn't care if Gabe was the greatest guy in the entire school — which he probably was — he still wasn't worth losing her mind over, or even losing a swim race.

"You know, this place is just like the girls' locker room," she finally sighed. "Almost."

"It probably smells worse."

She moved away from him and spied into the coaches' offices, which had been locked up with a metal grate. She shook the door.

Gabe turned and watched her. "Don't let Coach Kaplan catch you doing that."

"Why? What will he do?"

"Let's just say it involves lashes and a wet towel."

"Yow." She offered Gabe a smile, with one last hope that the whole mess would vanish into thin air.

Gabe kept watching her as she ran her hands along the metal grate. Finally he ran his hands through his hair and stood up. "Okay. I get the message, Kat. Let's go."

"Go where?"

"Go nowhere," he sighed. "Isn't that what you're trying to tell me, that you don't want to go out? That you want to say no?"

Kat held up her hands. "I wasn't going to say anything."

"You were, too. I can always tell."

"How?"

He began to smile, too. "Your mouth kind of trembles, like you're about to eat half my lunch or something."

"Hey, who always mooches whose lunch?" she pointed out. "Let's be honest here."

"Okay. Let's be honest!" Gabe stood up. "Great idea. You know, that's the best idea you've come up with in weeks."

Kat knew she had to tell him how she felt, even though she dreaded the consequences. She was ready for another big fight. She was ready for Gabe to ignore her for weeks. She was even ready for him to break off their radio partnership. What she wasn't ready for was plunging into some romance she was unsure about . . . and losing one of her best friends in the process.

She walked back down the aisle of lockers and faced him. She was shaking a little, but she somehow managed to form the words. "Okay, I'll say this once, and then I don't want to have to say it again. I like you, Gabe. A lot. Maybe even more than a lot. But I'm not ready for some heavy thing! Maybe I'll change my mind tomorrow; maybe I'll feel this way until graduation, I don't know. I'm sorry to keep saying I don't know, but I don't. That's just the way it is!"

She slumped down with her face in her hands and waited for Gabe's reaction. For a long time all she heard was the rustle of him gathering his things and the applause at the end of Mr. Melman's speech.

She didn't look up until she felt Gabe tap the top of her head. He was standing over her, his book bag slung over his shoulder, wearing a tired smile. "So what do you say we go hang out at the Wave tonight," he said. "Maybe we'll find out what's going on with Miranda."

"Are you serious?"

"You know, this hasn't been much easier on me than it has been on you," he admitted. "I've been dreading having you turn me down, but now that you've done it I think I'm kind of relieved. So let's go to the Wave, and I'll flirt with some freshmen, and you'll tell jokes, and maybe we'll walk home together . . . if we're both in the mood. How about it?"

"That's great," she sighed. She stood up and, without thinking, slipped her arms around his neck. Then she relaxed into the wonderful, familiar feel of his skin and hair.

"Hey, none of that," he joked, pushing her away. Nonetheless, he slipped his arm around her again as they walked out of the locker room. "You are making me crazy, Kat."

"Me?"

"Kat."

"Gaaaabe."

As soon as they were out the door, Gabe grabbed her in a wrestling hold, until she punched him in the side and they both started to run and laugh.

Down on Ocean Avenue, no one was laughing. Jojo was shivering. Jackson was scared. And Chip was staring across the street and into the arcade window.

"What now?" Jackson urged, after his tenth walk up and down Ocean Avenue. "We've looked everywhere. And there's no one in this fortune-teller's shop. It's been closed for hours. Chip, are you sure the note said for Miranda to meet Brent here?"

"Of course I'm sure," Chip said, squinting into the cold, wet air. He was staring into the arcade window again, catching the glint off Leanne's platinum hair as she leaned against the pinball machine.

"I could call Miranda's house one more time," Jojo suggested. She wove her arm through Jackson's and leaned her cheek against his shoulder. "Maybe somebody's home by now."

"Yeah, like her dad," Jackson replied. "Jojo, whatever's going on, I don't think Miranda wanted her dad to know. Otherwise he would have said something at the open house."

Chip stared into the arcade window again. "We're going to have to call her parents sometime."

"Unless we find her soon," Jackson said. "So that's what we have to do."

Chip didn't know if they'd find her or not. Of course he was worried and scared, too. But he wasn't only concerned with Miranda. Each time he'd walked up and down Ocean Avenue, he'd wanted to walk into the arcade and talk to Leanne. But he hadn't done it. How could he be so close and not even talk to her? It wasn't as if there was some kind of barrier at the arcade door, but there was still a line that Chip didn't know if he could cross. It wasn't his place at all.

His place, Chip thought, like Hud's school! Was he doing it again? Even with all the worry over Miranda, was he pegging his places and

Leanne's? His friends and hers, with a certain value judgment placed on each?

"Let's go across the street," Chip finally said, pushing down the lump of anger that still burned inside his chest.

"Into the arcade?" Jojo asked, as if he'd just suggested they take a dip in the freezing ocean.

"Leanne's in there. Maybe she can help."

"She is?" Jojo gasped. Then she shook her head. "Of course she is. Where else would she be? If you go in, you'd better leave me behind. Leanne won't want to see me."

Jackson reacted suddenly and grabbed her hand. "Chip's right, Jojo. We should go talk to her. Leanne might have seen something. Let's go to the arcade."

Jojo hesitated.

"Even if Leanne can't help, I want to go in and see her," Chip said. "I have to go in. We're not making any progress here."

Chip raced across the street before Jojo or Jackson could say anything else. He didn't realize that they'd followed him until he'd made his way through the blinking lights and funky crowd. He approached the pinball machine next to Leanne's, something called the Bomber Blast.

He put money in and played . . . badly.

Leanne made a few comments to a scruffy guy at the next machine until she finally caught sight of Chip. Her mouth fell open. She immediately put her head back down and began playing again.

Chip played, too. But his game was over almost as soon as he started.

"You're trying too hard," Leanne finally said, not looking at him.

"What?"

"Don't use so much force."

"Okay." He pulled the spring back more softly this time. Sure enough, the ball skated onto the board instead of ricochetting back down.

When Leanne looked at him again, she noticed Jojo and Jackson. Her face tensed up. "What is this, a raid?" She glared at Jojo. "Are you going to drag me home, or write another article for the paper?"

Jojo stepped toward her. "We need your help," she admitted. "We're looking for Miranda. Have you see her?"

Leanne bit her lip. Her hair fell over her face. She played the Cyclone for another minute, then pulled her hands away. Finally she answered, "I saw her. Brent, too. A while ago."

"You did see them?" Jackson gasped.

"Chip, tell Leanne about the note," Jojo insisted. "It's too important to keep it confidential."

Chip hesitantly repeated what he remembered of Brent's note, then touched Leanne's shoulder. "If you know anything about where Brent and Miranda might be, could you help us?"

"Please," Jojo added. "We need you."

Leanne moved away from the pinball machine. She looked from Chip to Jojo and back again. "The Wild Ride is at the amusement park. The place is closed. But I might be able to find someone who could get you in."

"Would you do that?" Jojo pleaded.

Leanne stared at Jojo. She stepped away from the pinball machine and took Chip's hand. "I guess I'll help," she finally said. "But only if you let me handle everything. Do you trust me enough to do that?"

Leanne looked at Chip, and then Chip looked back at Jackson and Jojo. Everyone looked pale and shaky in the weird orange/green light of the arcade. Somewhere an electronic bell was sounding and a pinball game had gone off on TILT.

"We trust you," Chip answered.

Jackson and Jojo nodded their heads.

Jojo believed in loyalty.

She believed in friendship.

And no matter how much she wanted to change — no matter how much she'd changed already — she would never have given up either of those two things.

She also knew that her heart was about to burst. She stood with Jackson at the entrance to the amusement park, while the man Leanne had found at the Pelican Coffee Shop — someone named McGyver — unlocked the main gate. Jackson stood close to her, but she sensed that he was far away. He wanted her advice, her company, but she had suddenly realized that she wasn't the one he'd been racing to find.

McGyver pushed open the heavy gate and ushered the four of them in. The park was like a ghost town. Jojo shivered at the faint sound of a boy's voice, coming eerily from the sky.

"You're right," McGyver said as soon as they entered the park. It was almost as if he could smell what was wrong and locate it exactly. "Somebody's in here. This way."

As they jogged to follow him, the hooting

grew louder. But it wasn't until they saw the Wild Ride that Jojo recognized Brent.

"Hey! YOOOOOOOO! WOOOO!" Brent was hollering.

He had seen them approach and was hanging out of the capsule to wave, almost as if he wanted to drop down so they could all watch his brains splatter on the pavement.

When Jackson saw Brent, he let go of Jojo and began to run. "WHERE IS SHE?" Jackson screamed. "IF SHE'S HURT, I'LL KILL YOU, TUCKER!!"

And that was when Jojo knew for sure. Her heart no longer felt as if it were going to burst. It was broken into a million pieces.

McGyver grabbed the control switch and the ride began to tilt, sending Brent back toward the ground. It wasn't until the capsule rested on the landing area that they even knew for sure that Miranda was inside. First Brent fell out, laughing hysterically as he fell off the platform. Then Miranda groped her way out, her hair across her face, her sweater torn.

Jojo made a move to comfort Miranda. But Jackson beat her to it. He swooped Miranda into his arms, kissing her hair, groping as Miranda wept and he clutched her.

Jojo waited. Miranda saw Jojo, tried to speak, but was too shaky to say anything.

"Let's get out of here," McGyver ordered, clamping a hand on Brent.

McGyver led the way, dragging Brent along with him. Chip and Leanne followed, their hands linked. Then came Jackson and Miranda, leaning against each other, arms clutching each other's waist. Lastly, Jojo walked alone.

Jackson paused once to glance back at Jojo.

I like you. I respect you, Jackson's eyes said to her, but I'm sorry. Miranda is still the one.

Jojo put her head down as tears poured from her eyes.

FIFTEEN

Revenge.

It was hard to think about revenge at the Wave Cafe. The food smelled too good. The music was too tight. Everyone in the place looked too happy to be there, especially after enduring the endless open house at school. Kat and Gabe were joking up a storm. Even Simon Wheeldon, who stood by himself nursing an orange soda, seemed glad to be there. Brandy had her coke and onion rings and ketchup in front of her, and Lisa had her diet soda and curly fries.

So Brandy didn't see how revenge could quite be the theme for the evening's discussion between her and Lisa. In fact it sounded more like a homework assignment. You know, *In an essay of 500 words or less, explore your feelings about the personal theme of revenge. . . .*

Right.

Brandy had to explore her personal feelings about using this favor to get revenge on Jojo. What would she do to her? How would she make Jojo pay? What exactly would she ask for?

"What do you want, Brandy?" Lisa said, as if on cue. She had thrown her ever-present makeup bag up on the table, next to the fries. It flashed in Brandy's mind that Lisa's new lipstick color looked a lot like the ketchup. Brandy didn't mention it. She just shrugged.

"I don't know," Brandy answered.

Lisa sighed and then wrinkled her nose. "You are so hard to pin down, Brandy. I have given you an opportunity a million girls would die for."

Brandy shrugged again. It wasn't as if Lisa had given her a date with a hunk like Brent Tucker. It was hard to imagine a million girls lining up just to have Jojo Hernandez owe them a favor, especially now that Jojo was such a big deal at school. Was Brandy supposed to ask if she could move in with Jojo, too? *Puleeze.*

"So what are you going to ask for?" Lisa prompted.

"I don't know. Maybe to give me some of her clothes?"

Lisa looked as if she were going to slap

Brandy. "That is such small thinking," she said.

"Why? Jojo has great clothes. At least she used to, before she started pretending to be Mother Teresa."

Lisa laughed.

Brandy folded her arms. She didn't feel like eating anymore. All the questions that Lisa had asked about Jojo seemed too hard to answer — too complex, too nerve-racking, too weird. Just like Brandy's feelings about Jojo. Jojo was the one girl who'd been born with cheerleader stamped on her forehead. She almost never seemed to force the spirit or the attitude. Brandy, on the other hand, always felt as if her position as head cheerleader was pretty iffy. If Karen Miller hadn't slipped on the waxy gym floor during the tryouts, then she would have ended up as number one, not Brandy.

But Lisa always insisted that none of that mattered. Taking advantage of your opportunities was everything to her.

"I decided to do you a favor," Lisa informed Brandy. She finally put her makeup bag away and laid her purse between the onion rings and the drinks. She fished around and produced a piece of computer paper, almost exactly like the one Simon had used for their statement against

Brent. She handed the paper to Brandy, taking care not to get a spot of food on it.

Brandy turned the page around and read it. It *was* like the sheet that Simon had drawn up. But this page stated the deal between Jojo and Brandy:

> *Agreed upon this day by Jojo and Brandy a contract for the following:*
>
> **Bought** — *from Brandy, information against Brent Tucker, to be used for publication in the school paper.*
>
> **Owed** — *by Jojo, one favor, to be selected by Brandy at her discretion.*
>
> *Signed,*
>
> _____ *Brandy Kurtz*
> _____ *Jojo Hernandez*

"And I used to wonder if I would ever use anything I'd learned in computer class," Lisa giggled. She ripped off the dotted border with glee.

Brandy wasn't sure how to react. Signing the paper against Brent was bad enough, but this was really pushing things. Now there would be no going back. Even if she and Jojo made up and became buddy-buddy again, Brandy would have to ask Jojo to pay up anyway.

Just then Lisa reached across and pinned Brandy's arm to the tabletop. Brandy looked in the direction Lisa was pointing and at the same time read the silently mouthed letters that were emerging from Lisa's lips: J–O–J–O.

It was Jojo all right, wandering around the cafe as if she were stumbling along the dark, foggy beach. Her hair was completely frizzed. Her face looked pale and sunken. She was walking away from Kat, who went back into repeating her KHOT routines for the adoring crowd.

"Go and give Jojo the paper," Lisa ordered. "She needs to know before that article about Brent comes out. She needs to know that she made a deal, and she's really going to have to pay. Tell her to read it and weep."

Brandy pushed her chair back over the sawdust on the floor, then wound around tables, passing the jukebox and statue of King Neptune. She walked right up to Jojo.

Jojo barely even noticed her. Up close Brandy could see that Jojo looked truly troubled and weary. Brandy had never seen her look like that.

Brandy almost threw the paper away. But then she glanced back at Lisa, who was following her every move. She pushed Lisa's paper in Jojo's face.

"What is this?" Jojo asked in a hazy voice.

"Read it and see," she answered. Brandy couldn't say read it and weep, because there were already tears in Jojo's eyes. "It's part of a deal we made with Simon Wheeldon. One good favor deserves another."

Jojo skimmed the contract, then threw her head back in an unbelieving moan. "Is this for real?"

"You bet it is," Brandy glared. "Now what do you have to say?"

Jojo looked around the cafe again, until her eyes settled on Simon, who was still sipping his orange drink. "I only have one thing to say," Jojo managed. "Thanks a lot, Simon Wheeldon."

After stuffing the paper into her pocket, Jojo turned around and left the Wave. Once she was on the planks of the pier again, she realized that the fog had made everything look surreal. Hey, her evening had certainly been surreal. Maybe her entire life was nothing but a fuzzy, painful dream.

She leaned over the railing, letting her tears fall from her cheeks into the water. After Miranda had been rescued from the Wild Ride, Jojo had known she wasn't needed — or wanted — so she'd left Jackson and Miranda alone to work things out. Then Chip and Leanne had wandered off, and Jojo certainly hadn't wanted to hang around while that McGyver guy tried to scare Brent Tucker with threats he was never going to carry out.

So Jojo had started to walk home, heading through the fog as blindly as if it were a white-out. But before she'd even crossed the pier, she'd known that she wasn't ready to go back to her cheery, straightforward parents and her nice, neat house.

For the first time in Jojo's life she wished that her life could be nice and straightforward again. She'd sobbed because she couldn't remember what it was like to have anything cheery and neat. If she'd wanted to find a new Jojo, she'd certainly succeeded. And now there was no going back to a time before things were messy . . . before she'd fallen in love with the boy who loved one of her best friends.

Finally Jojo had stepped into the Wave, where she'd told Kat that Miranda was all right. Kat and Gabe had gone back to their jokes, pretending to fight and banter, but really being as tight as Leanne was with Chip . . . or Jackson was with Miranda. Jojo had stood in the middle of the music and the Friday night party, until she'd been handed the letter bomb by Brandy, which was the ultimate proof that the old, uncomplicated Jojo was a person of the past. As to the future Jojo . . . maybe Brandy was the only one who knew the answer to that one.

"Brandy," Jojo trembled, turning away from the water and brushing aside another tear. "All I need is to owe Brandy something."

She faced the ocean again, when the sound of a badly tuned car motor thrust itself through the fog. Tires thumped on the wooden pier. Headlights created fuzzy white circles. Then the engine shifted gears, and a boy called out to her.

"Can I give you a ride?"

Jojo ignored him, assuming that it was some creep, until something clicked deep in her consciousness. Suddenly she recognized the horrendous car, the salesman's voice. It wasn't just any creep, it was Simon Wheeldon, next to Brent Tucker the biggest creep in Crescent Bay.

Sure, I want a ride, she said to herself, her despair flipping over into fury. She stomped

over a few planks and sure enough, there was
Simon at the wheel of the grossest car Jojo had
ever seen.

She climbed in, too angry to say anything besides, "Take me home. Twelve blocks up Ocean
Avenue."

He drove, obviously startled by being treated
like a taxi driver. "Are you all right?" he finally
asked when they stopped at a red light.

Jojo felt the pressure of tears again. A few
leaked down her cheeks.

"Did something happen with you and the
newspaper guy?" Simon asked in a shy voice.

"What?"

The light turned green. Simon tapped the
steering wheel as he drove. "Maybe he's not the
only guy for you," Simon said. "Maybe there's
somebody even better just waiting for you to
notice him."

Give me a break! Jojo almost screamed. What
she did not need that night was romantic advice
from knife-in-the-back Simon!

He turned onto her street, then pulled over
across the street from her house. "I know a guy
who'd do anything for you," he said, as soon as
he stopped the car. "Whatever you need, he'd
try to help you get it."

Jojo was about to tell him off when it dawned on her. Simon adored her, just as she adored Jackson. Simon may have ruined her future, but he'd only done it to make her like him.

She no longer had the heart to rail at him. She was too tired and too sympathetic. "That's okay, Simon," she said in her kindest voice. "Thanks for the ride."

Jojo didn't even slam the door after getting out. She slowly walked up the driveway, no longer crying. Simon sat in his car watching after her until long after she'd gone in the front door.

Late that night, Jojo was dreaming about the Wild Ride. She was being thrown up and down. Miranda wasn't with her. Nor was Brent. Or Jackson. Jojo was all alone, holding on for her life as the ride flung her around the foggy sky.

Clunk. Tap, tap, tap.

Someone was knocking on the outside of the capsule, even as it continued to swing. Jojo still held on, until the tapping sound grew louder and she realized she was covered with sweat. She clawed the sheet away from her face and sat up, trembling until she realized that someone was knocking at her bedroom door.

"Jojo?"

"Come in," Jojo whispered.

The door slowly opened. Leanne stood in the shadow of the hall light, her hair glimmering as if she were some kind of witch . . . but a good witch, with a graceful, friendly expression.

"I'm sorry to wake you," Leanne said. "I thought you'd still be up."

"No."

"I just wanted you to know that I was back," Leanne told her. "And that I was glad your friend was okay."

Jojo rubbed her eyes. "Thanks for your help."

"If you ever need my help again, just ask." Leanne tapped the door frame. "Okay?"

"Sure." Jojo nodded.

Leanne nodded back. For one long, drawn-out moment the two girls looked at one another. Then Leanne closed Jojo's door, Jojo's head dropped onto her pillow, and she fell into a deep, peaceful sleep.

Don't miss book #5 *Staying Cool* in the sizzling series:

TOTALLY HOT!

Gabe Sachs concentrates on keeping his cool around KHOT radio partner, Kat McDonough. But it's not easy. One minute Kat's hanging all over him and the next minute she's giving him the brush-off. Gabe's sick of riding Kat's emotional roller coaster. But if he gets off now, will he lose the only girl he has ever truly loved?

Lovebirds Miranda and Jackson can't get enough of each other since they've finally reunited. And their public displays of affection are making Miranda's ex, Eric Geraci, and love-spurned Jojo Hernandez nauseous. Do broken hearts ever heal?

Meanwhile gorgeous, calculating Brent Tucker has figured out a way to force Kat to go out with him. And Chip and Leanne are heating things up *in* school and *out*!

point®

Other books you will enjoy, about real kids like you!

☐ MZ43469-1	**Arly** Robert Newton Peck	$2.95
☐ MZ40515-2	**City Light** Harry Mazer	$2.75
☐ MZ44494-8	**Enter Three Witches** Kate Gilmore	$2.95
☐ MZ40943-3	**Fallen Angels** Walter Dean Myers	$3.50
☐ MZ40847-X	**First a Dream** Maureen Daly	$3.25
☐ MZ43020-3	**Handsome as Anything** Merrill Joan Gerber	$2.95
☐ MZ43999-5	**Just a Summer Romance** Ann M. Martin	$2.75
☐ MZ44629-0	**Last Dance** Caroline B. Cooney	$2.95
☐ MZ44628-2	**Life Without Friends** Ellen Emerson White	$2.95
☐ MZ42769-5	**Losing Joe's Place** Gordon Korman	$2.95
☐ MZ43664-3	**A Pack of Lies** Geraldine McCaughrean	$2.95
☐ MZ43419-5	**Pocket Change** Kathryn Jensen	$2.95
☐ MZ43821-2	**A Royal Pain** Ellen Conford	$2.95
☐ MZ44429-8	**A Semester in the Life of a Garbage Bag** Gordon Korman	$2.95
☐ MZ43867-0	**Son of Interflux** Gordon Korman	$2.95
☐ MZ43971-5	**The Stepfather Game** Norah McClintock	$2.95
☐ MZ41513-1	**The Tricksters** Margaret Mahy	$2.95
☐ MZ43638-4	**Up Country** Alden R. Carter	$2.95

Watch for new titles coming soon!
Available wherever you buy books, or use this order form.

Scholastic Inc., P.O. Box 7502, 2931 E. McCarty Street, Jefferson City, MO 65102

Please send me the books I have checked above. I am enclosing $ _____
Please add $2.00 to cover shipping and handling. Send check or money order - no cash or C.O.D's please.

Name _____

Address _____

City _____ State/Zip _____

Please allow four to six weeks for delivery. Offer good in U.S.A. only. Sorry, mail orders are not available to residents of Canada. Prices subject to changes.

PNT691